Savage Control

A Dark Omegaverse Science Fiction Romance

The Controllers
Book 10

L.V. Lane

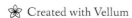 Created with Vellum

Contents

Prologue

Theta was the first dynamic to be revealed in a human infected with the Copper virus. A junior research assistant accidentally infected himself, or so it was alleged. Thetas are hyper-intelligent and driven toward the accumulation of wealth, prestige, or both.

Of all the dynamics, I believe the theta dynamic to be the most ruthless.

My wealth of personal experience has supported this conclusion.

~ Doctor Lillian Brach

The remote spaceport, Kix29

Abby

"Have you ever met a delta?" Jenna asked as our ship prepared to dock at Kix29, a space station in the middle of nowhere that was soon to be my temporary home.

The transport I'd been taking to Tolis, a perfectly habitable planet, had suffered multiple technical failures. I tried to ignore that I was floating around space in a hunk of metal that had problems, but it was hard when you wore magnetic boots because the artificial gravity kept failing.

I shuddered.

"I thought gammas liked deltas?" Jenna asked, distracting me from my space phobia.

"I don't know much about them," I said honestly, focused on the small portal window we were standing beside, through which I could see the station umbilical heading toward our ship. The transport juddered as the metallic clips locked us into place. Kix29 wasn't much better than a transport, just a bigger lump of metal floating around in the void of space now that I thought about it.

"You're really freaked out," she said, smiling now.

"I am," I admitted. "I was supposed to be on Tolis a week ago."

Jenna was one of life's adventurers. A lota dynamic, she personified the caste with her unbridled curiosity for everything in life. We'd met during the two-week transit.

"I started reading about them after I met you," she said. "Sounds fascinating. Did you know they have a hook?"

"I, ah, did hear about the hook." Heard about it and dismissed it. Clearly it was anatomically ridiculous. I mean, the alpha knot made sense, since some animals had them. "I've never met a delta. I don't suppose I ever will."

"What about the online forums, where you can" —she started giggling— "hook up with them. Ever been tempted?"

I *hadn't* heard about the online forums. I shook my head slowly, but my lips tugged up. "That sounds terrible."

"Why?" She shrugged. "Apparently, it's very pleasurable. Well, it's also really kinky. All kinds of hot and steamy stuff goes on. Did you know they're together? Deltas share everything, including each other and their chosen gamma."

"I've never thought about that side of it," I said because, unlike Jenna, I wasn't curious, at least not about deltas.

"It's all there in the paper I read last night," she said. "I should have been sleeping, but sleep is so overrated. Lillian Brach, she's a famous omega who used to be in charge of the viral research program until her theta subordinate snatched the top job. Thetas, they just can't help themselves, full of elitist ideology. They really don't play well with others. I've read plenty about omegas, and contrary to popular opinion, there is nothing to suggest they lose all mental acumen the moment they reveal." She huffed out a breath and rolled her eyes. "Sorry, I'm getting distracted. Where was I? Oh, yes! Deltas. It was Lillian Brach's paper—very detailed, and absolutely fascinating. You should read it sometime."

I nodded vaguely, trying to catch up with all of that. I hadn't mentioned that my parents were thetas. People tended to look at you funny when you said anything about knowing one in real life. And she was right—thetas kept to themselves and had a superiority complex a mile wide. My parents were comparably measured examples of the dynamic, while my older brother was closer to the god complex end of the spectrum. They didn't really mix with other dynamics, although all dynamics were guilty to some extent of gravitating toward their own, except gammas, who were the rarest. Mixing with our own wasn't practical. I'd never met either a gamma or delta.

"The hook part is just a rumor though," I said confidently. I couldn't imagine a viral doctor paying credence to gossip. I might never have met a delta, but I'd met plenty of alphas, and allegedly, deltas were much like them. More likely, it was the deltas themselves who'd started the ridiculous story.

"About the hook? Oh no, that's definitely not a rumor." She shook her head vehemently.

What?!

"A lot of safety checks," she said, indicating the portal window and the umbilical cord connecting us with the station. A loud hiss signified that the umbilical had finally docked and the hatch had opened.

Meanwhile, I was having a minor mental breakdown about the delta hook. It had to be small, right? Where would it even go?

I shuffled forward under the swell of bodies that sought to exit the ship.

"I'll send you the details of that hookup site," she said, winking dramatically. "I can tell you're curious now."

"Please don't." I shook my head, although I was laughing too. They were really the worst source of humorous material.

We made our way along the umbilical and onto the sturdier space station. Several thousand people lived on Kix29, supporting the mining operation and the local planet below. I would be stuck here for a week until a ship bound for Tolis arrived, while Jenna was heading for Ridious and shipping straight out.

Jenna hefted her backpack higher onto her shoulder before offering me a wave. "If you ever meet a delta, I definitely want the details. Take care, Abby."

Chapter One

Jordan

I had a feeling the skinny beta prick was cheating me as I watched the hands being played. Kade was knocking back drinks like it was an Awakening Day celebration, but I wasn't in the mood.

The spaceport, Kix29, was situated in the Sirius system, supporting a substantive mining operation. They liked to claim they were part of the Empire, but in truth, it was fringe.

How the fuck had we ended up here?

A long fucking story, but I suspected our boss' hacker friend had something to do with it.

This whole operation had been bullshit from the start. My skin was itching, but I got like this sometimes.

The only thing that would make me relax was beating the shit out of someone.

The skinny beta was looking like a promising candidate.

Yeah, I understood that I was unhinged. A lifetime of

therapy couldn't sort my demons out, not that I was interested in discussing my feelings with anyone. I figured there was no point in trying, so I might as well embrace the dark and all that jazz. The bouts of insomnia weren't ideal, but they hadn't killed me yet. A few other people might have died because of my less than congenial mood swings, but hey, they'd had it coming.

Kade kicked me under the table.

"Got that eye twitch going on there, buddy," he said, smirking.

I scowled at the fucker, although he didn't lift his eyes from his hand of cards. Little punk knew that was baiting.

My communicator bleeped, so I excused myself from the next round, rising from the table where five other players sat smoking and drinking, and clipped my earbud in.

"*What the fuck are you doing in Sirius?*" Lucian demanded. Our boss was a straight talking alphahole with more money than god and a snarky attitude if things didn't go to his exact plans.

He also had a hacker in his pocket that we'd nicknamed the Gecko because the freak was always going on about them and who delighted in making my life hell. I'd never met the Gecko, but I'd be sure to acquaint him with my fist if I ever did.

"Ask your dickhead gecko lover," I snapped. I wasn't one for mincing words either—not always the best approach with Lucian, but given he was light years away, I felt safe to vent.

"*I'm gonna strangle the fuck,*" Lucian snarled. I didn't need the visual to know he would be prowling back and forth in front of the windowed wall that looked out onto his club, likely wearing a smart dark suit, hair impeccable. Depending on the time of day, a couple of beta pets might be waiting to attend to Lucian's every need. Peppermint Moon catered to the dynamic elites and wannabes—just one of many interests the corrupt business mogul had on his books.

"You're gonna need to get in the queue," I replied. My eyes were on the table, where Kade was tossing down another lost hand. "We'll be back in a week. Due to ship out tomorrow."

"*Got the package?*" Lucian asked, all business again.

"Yeah, we got the package. Let's hope it's worth this bullshit."

"*Fine then,*" Lucian said, and the communication closed out.

"Do you know any computer hackers?" I turned back to the table and pinned the slimy beta clearing up the shiny credits with a look.

"H-Hacker?" Bobby, Bobbit, Bobbin? Whatever the fuck his name was, he gave a telling stutter in his vague response. He didn't know a hacker, but he was up to something here and had guilt written all over his face.

My eyes narrowed on the squirming man.

"Fuck, Jordan," Kade muttered. "Can you give it a rest? He's not here. These are real cards. Drop it, will you?"

My head swung in Kade's direction.

He raised both hands in silent surrender. "Whatever," he said. "Sorry, guys, we're out."

His chair scraped across the floor as he stood and pushed out the door.

I pinned Bob the beta with a glare before pivoting and stomping after Kade.

"You don't need to be a dick all the time," Kade said as I fell in step beside him.

I didn't answer. He was mouthy when he'd had a drink, and I'd learned not to rise to the bait. He was built like a tank, so beating on him was spectacularly unrewarding.

"One of us needs to be a dick, or you'd have your ass handed to you daily."

Okay, I'd gone there. We were deltas, a complicated dynamic. We were *rare*.

I was five years older than Kade. We'd both come through the orphan's program on Chimera, the unwanted offspring of a drug addict and alcoholic.

Kade's mother was a drug addict, but he didn't do drugs.

My father was an alcoholic, but I didn't drink. We both had plenty of other vices, so it wasn't like we were missing out.

I was a lost soul until the day Kade's scrawny ass was dumped in the home by law enforcement after they'd found his mother dead. He'd wanted to fight everyone, tried it too. He was nine, and I'd been fourteen. I'd let the little punk wear himself out by beating on me every day in the gym.

He'd had a lot of anger, but I didn't care. I'd found my missing piece, and we'd been inseparable ever since.

That was the thing about deltas—we were always in pairs. Part of that was because we were rare, and part was because of our unusual situation regarding our most compatible dynamic partner.

Kade stopped abruptly.

"Did you hear that?"

I stopped too. "Hear what?" Before he could answer, my communicator beeped, and a voice that made me want to pummel on the owner said, "*Incoming. It's about to get busy.*"

I fucking hated the Gecko, but there were times when he was useful...

The spaceport alarms blared, and orange ceiling lights began to flash.

"What the fuck is happening?" I snarled into the communicator.

"*Raiders,*" Lucian's hacker said.

Abby

The spaceport, Kix29, in the distant corner of the Sirius system, supported the mining operations here. The location was almost fringe.

Okay, I was trying to make myself feel better. It was definitely fringe.

How had I, a therapist employed by the military, ended up here?

It was a long and complex story that began with an emergency diversion on a simple transit from one base to another during a three-month field trip, compounded by bad luck and a spectacular level of transport failures, and resulted in me being galactic miles away from my intended destination.

I should be in Chimera now, sipping on a latte between clients.

Instead, I was eating questionable food in a space canteen, surrounded by rough-looking mining personnel. I was used to the military, so it wasn't that much of a stretch, but the whole place had an edge, like it was on the verge of catastrophe, and it was making me nervous.

I'd been stuck here for a week—a very long week.

I should have been shipping out today, but I'd just gotten news that I would be stuck here for another week.

The canteen was always busy. Thousands of people lived on this station permanently, and docked vessels could swell that number. Dozens of functional white tables and bench seating were lined up in rows, with a service area dispensing food along one wall and the cleanup area for after on the left. I'd found a seat in the middle because it made for a faster exit, and the less time I spent in here, the better.

On days like today, I questioned my career choice. My parents were both thetas and had been disappointed that I didn't similarly reveal. Being a therapist and helping others was not a path they could understand in the broadest terms, but if I was going to be a therapist, only the highest, most elite kind would meet my parent's expectations. The best paying customer, courtesy of the never-ending war against the Uncorrupted, was the military command on Chimera.

So here I was awaiting spare parts that were due in the next five days, unlikely to leave for Chimera in potentially another week, and bored out of my mind.

There was no such thing as day or night on the station, only endless, artificial, twenty-four-hour cycles broken into shifts. I missed natural air and the feeling of solid ground beneath my feet, especially since the springy, metallic floors and walls that predominated such stations made me feel at sea. I also missed my work, which was varied and interesting, with a good mix of other dynamics who were part of the Empire's ever evolving military machine.

But as the alarm blared for the third time today, I would have gladly settled for a job somewhere mundane, with poor career opportunities that didn't involve space travel...and specifically, finding myself on a remote spaceport with not even a token military presence.

The alarm continued a few seconds before cutting off, and then everyone went back to eating like this was perfectly normal. Perhaps it was. I had been here a week, and it sounded at least once a day. I'd be a nervous wreck if I stayed here much longer.

No sooner had it stopped than it started, again.

I glanced around the canteen at my fellow diners, meeting similar expressions of confusion.

"I don't think this is another drill," the beta male sitting two seats down from me said when the alarm continued to issue a *bleep-bleep* warning.

We were supposed to be safe. When the vessel limped into the space dock, I'd been told it had a state-of-the-art defense system that would protect us from our enemy, the Uncorrupted.

I was a gamma, which the virus revealed to me when I was seventeen. The Uncorrupted wanted to eradicate the virus. If they breached the station, I would be captured, taken away, and experimented on in their quest to find a contagion that would target others of my kind.

There were many and varied stories, both official and unofficial, about the Uncorrupted's plans. None of them filled me with glee.

The *bleep-bleep* changing to a *whoop-whoop* tipped ice into my veins. Overhead, amber lights began flashing in the ceiling.

I shared a look with the beta, rising from my seat and hoping this was simply a more comprehensive drill.

There were two double door exits from the canteen, and I'd started to head for the ones on my left when the alarm abruptly ceased.

I froze.

Another glitch in the system, maybe? After the previous false alarms, collective groans went up.

Staring at my tray of half eaten food, I wondered if I should tidy it up. A few people had sat back down, but the clink of cutlery and the chatter around me felt off. I didn't feel like eating anymore. When no instructions nor explanation came, I grabbed my tray and headed for the disposal.

The double doors to my right suddenly slammed open, and a man in a brown flight suit, typical of the haulage operations, burst into the room. "Raaiddders!"

A blast sounded, a hole opened up in his chest, blood splattered, and his body collapsed facedown.

The tray dropped from my nerveless fingers to hit the floor with a crash. The lights cut to emergency mode, bathing the room in an eerie green glow as the collective occupants of the canteen ran in a crazed mob, fleeing for the opposite door.

I went with them, swept along in the rush. The row of tables and benches made obstacles of the worst kind as the emergency lights began to strobe erratically. Someone pushed me, shoving an elbow or fist to the center of my back. The blow sent me sprawling, and I landed in an ungraceful heap, where boots of stampeding staff pounded me back down. I scrambled to my feet, only to be bowled over again. My chin smacked against a bench. I bit my tongue and tasted blood.

The *put-put* of automatic weapons sounded unbearably loud through the screams and the ringing in my ears.

I staggered up for the second time and ran a zigzag path between the benches for the exit. People fell beside me, bullets tearing into flesh and sending great arcs of blood across the white furniture, floors, walls...and me.

The blood of ordinary people whose only mistake was to be present at this station.

The blood of people who were now dead or desperately injured and soon to be dead.

I didn't want to be dead. I was too young, and there was too much I wanted to do with my life. I just wanted to live.

Blood made the floor slick and treacherous, and I skidded through the exit door, hitting the corridor wall so hard, I bounced off it. Dots swam before my eyes, and blood pooled in my mouth, where I'd bitten my tongue. Bullets tore up the wall beside me, twisting metal and sending sparks shooting. I pressed off the wall, dashing to the left, where the corridor led to the personnel quarters.

Most people veered right toward the docks, but I was committed to mindless flight mode and my legs only understood *run*.

Another double door waited ahead. A pace away, it sprang apart, and two huge men barreled through. The black formfitting uniform said they were security of some kind, maybe even soldiers. They were tall and built. Alphas, I thought. Conscription was mandatory, and they were invariably deployed in the war, which was odd because I hadn't seen any alphas, military or otherwise, while stuck on this godforsaken space station.

Maybe a military vessel had docked? I felt my spirits lift.

The alpha on the left was dark blond, while the right-hand alpha's hair was dark brown. Both were sinfully handsome... Death at the hands of a raider might've been imminent, but I still found the time to notice they were hot.

My legs started backpedaling, and my hands shot out. The dark-haired alpha's eyes widened before my body crumpled into his.

I thought for a split second that he'd been a figment of my imagination and that I'd run straight into another wall.

"Whoa," he murmured.

"Fuck!" the other said. "We need to back the fuck up."

Fingers bit into my arm as dark and handsome shoved me behind his back just as gunfire opened up.

A terrifying battle cry came from the food court's direction, a cross between a scream and a whoop. Ice flooded my veins, and my already frantic heart rate took another spike.

I couldn't see what was happening around the towering alpha's body. The world became a chaotic kaleidoscope that moved fast, then slow. More people surged into the corridor, their screams and shouts ripping into me as surely as a bullet.

"Shit!" the one holding my arm said. That was all the

15

warning I got before he spun around and shoved me through the double doors he'd just entered by.

"This is your fucking fault, Kade!" the blond man rumbled at the darker one still fisting my arm.

The closing door shut out some, but not all, of the cacophony.

"My fault?! Like I'm responsible for raiders turning up. Don't be a dick!" Kade, as I now knew him, snarled back.

Bullets reverberated off the closed doors beside us. My eyes shifted from Kade to his blond sidekick to the flimsy barrier between us and certain death.

"If you hadn't insisted we spend our night drinking and playing cards, we might've had something more effective than this popgun." Blondie waved the small handheld about while regarding it with open disgust. "I'm too old for this staying up all night bullshit. We should've been in the dock already."

I'd spent most of my adult life studying human psychology, so I recognized crazy when I saw it. Only *I* could have the misfortune to be intercepted by two insane alphas. "This is not the time—"

"Too old! For fuck's sake, Jordan," Kade continued, talking right over me like there wasn't an attack happening and our lives weren't on the line. "You're like five years older than me. That's a long way off fucking old!" He turned and shot out the lock to the double doors beside us, and a safety deadbolt dropped with a mighty thud.

A sharp, terror steeped squeal escaped my lips. I tried to pry his fingers from my arm, since they were cutting off the circulation and the owner was clearly a pickle short of a picnic, as my grandma used to say.

"Not happening, sweetheart," he said while glaring at the other man.

"Well, you act like you're prepubescent most of the fucking time!" Jordan, aka blondie, snapped back.

I was inclined to side with Jordan at this stage...and I really wanted my arm back.

"We need to leave," I said. I considered myself a true pacifist, but I was ready to stab something vital if he didn't let me go.

Both heads swung my way, and just like that, the tension took on a whole new dimension.

Chapter Two

Kade

The base was under attack. Raiders were shooting up the place, and as much as I hated to agree with what Jordan said—because he was a cocky bastard at the best of times—we needed better weapons.

Oh, and the tiny woman who had just plowed into me was hot as fuck.

I got it, we were under attack, and no, I shouldn't have been thinking with my dick, but with full respect to the situation, how long did it take to notice that a woman was hot? Microseconds—that was how long.

She had short, pixie-cropped brown hair, huge blue eyes hidden behind dark-rimmed glasses, a little heart-shaped face... and the most disgustingly shapeless dress I'd ever seen. I wasn't letting the stunningly bad clothing choice put me off. She'd been plastered against me for long enough for me to notice the soft plumpness of tits and to get a fair impression about the rest —petite, but with curves. I liked curves, a lot.

Jordan was giving her a not very subtle eye fuck, trying to figure out what was going on underneath the green sack she was wearing. Tough luck, buddy. She'd smacked into me, and I was calling dibs.

Lips tightening, he gave me his best steely glare.

I smirked because I really was an immature prick sometimes.

"I guess we're going the other way," he said, frowning at the door I'd just blasted locked. We'd both known that way wasn't an option, even before the bundle of smock covered woman crashed into us. I couldn't hear much of what was happening on the other side, but I'd seen enough to know we would get our asses handed to us if we tried to go that way. "We need to find somewhere safe for..." I turned and gave her an expectant look. Jordan huffed out a snort at my blatant play.

She flicked a nervous look at Jordan, who was giving off his menacing vibes and had probably just rolled his eyes, before turning back to me. "Abby," she said.

Cogs were turning behind those glasses. I got a weird impression that hottie was psychoanalyzing me. Trained therapists couldn't straighten out all my kinks, although I had nothing on Jordan.

"Somewhere safe for Abby," I continued.

Jordan tapped his ear communicator. I'd left mine back at our quarters because I tended to lose them when I'd had a drink. "We're overrun and on the wrong side of a locked door leading to the docks. What are our options?" Jordan's eyes suddenly narrowed, and his nostrils flared. "We've got a civilian with us. Now is not the time to be a dick."

I could feel Abby's arm trembling under my fingers as she glanced at me in question. I tried for a reassuring smile. "Just a bit of banter," I said, winking.

"I swear to fucking god," Jordan said, pitching straight into a rant. "I will reach down this communicator and rip out your fucking throat."

I grimaced. He was never much for finesse. "He's a bit rough around the edges. Don't mind it," I said to Abby

"Two small handguns liberated from a couple of raiders," Jordan said, tone clipped like he was hanging onto his patience by a thread. He puffed air out of flared nostrils much like an angry bull. "Yes, I know I should have been better prepared. You've had the pair of us on a merry chase for this fucking package. Lucian will be pissed if he doesn't get it or us back, so figure something out.

"Yes," Jordan said tersely. "And no, I'm not describing her eye color, asshole!"

I smirked. Nosy assed hacker.

Jordan suddenly swung to look over his shoulder at a security camera. "You're on a warning," he said. "Fuck this up, and I will tear apart every floor in that building until I find the grubby hole where you play at god. Lucian doesn't employ us for our conversational skills. Give me half a reason, and I'll acquaint you with some of them."

He swung back to me and nodded once. "We can handle it, since it's not like we have a fucking choice." To Abby, he said, "A military vessel is being redirected. We need to hole up somewhere and sit this out. Raiders like to have sport, but they pack up and ship out at the first sign of challenge. The lab and the agriculture pods haven't activated their drop doors. If we can get to one of them, we'll be safe enough."

"If?" Abby asked. Her pretty Cupid's bow lips were trembling. Fuck knows what she did here. Really, her clothing choice was so bad, I couldn't imagine it was people facing, but she'd latched onto the crux of the statement in a flash and clearly, she wasn't stupid.

"We have support," Jordan said, ignoring her question.

His eyes lowered slowly, suggesting he was trying to assess what was under her green smock before realizing what he was doing and dragging them up again. "Our guy has access to the internal cameras. He can help to guide us away from danger. I'm not going to lie to you, there are some places where it's going to get tricky, but if we stay focused, there's every chance we can get through this. Are you up for that, Abby?"

"Yes," she said. "Yes, I'm definitely up for that."

Jordan nodded once. "We're going to need to move fast."

"Good," she said. "Whatever it takes. I don't want to die. Whatever you need me to do, I'll do it."

"Good girl," Jordan said approvingly.

We took off down the corridor at a jog, under the drone of the alarm and the eerie green emergency lighting, Jordan at the front, Abby in the middle, and me at the rear. For a little thing, and despite the cumbersome smock, she had no problem keeping up.

I didn't care much about where somebody was from, whether they were rich or poor or anything else. A person's attitude got them through life. Life had served me some rough cards, and I mostly didn't think about it...until days like today, when someone who'd likely never been subject to the ugly side of the universe showed their spirit under pressure. Abby didn't hesitate, balk, or succumb to hysterics. No, she just got on with it.

I could tell she was a fighter.

At the end of the corridor, we turned left. Distant gunfire and screams echoed off the walls. Ahead or behind, it was hard to tell. We took the next right.

At the next T-junction, Jordan slowed to a stop. His faraway look said he was talking to the Gecko.

Jordan

"*Casualties ahead,*" the Gecko said. "*No movement, so I'm going with dead. Three civilians, and one that might be a raider or security. The rest are behind a drop door.*"

"Stay close but alert until I check," I said to Kade.

The three bodies lay prone, spilling out of a room on our right, their white lab coats splattered with copious amounts of blood. One wore a black and gray uniform that I thought might have been security or base personnel of some kind.

"Don't look," Kade cautioned Abby as he came to a stop beside me. For all we knew, some of these people were her former friends.

I made the mistake of glancing up to find Abby in Kade's arms. I met her wide-eyed stare briefly before Kade hauled her close. My eyes lowered to where her small hand fisted his T-shirt. The universe was full of violence and trauma, but some people were meant to be protected from it, and I could tell from fifty paces that Abby was one of them.

I knelt and flipped the guy in gray over, grunting in disgust when I found a pulse beam holstered. The idiot hadn't even drawn his weapon. I liberated it and checked it over.

"*Incoming from behind,*" the Gecko said.

"Let's move," I said as the sound of automatic fire drew closer. I set a fast pace, knowing Kade would call it if Abby had problems. He didn't call, so I was guessing whatever she'd seen before plowing into Kade had provided a powerful motivation.

"*Take a left at the next T*," the Gecko said. "*The group behind you has turned off.*"

"Good," I muttered. There was an itch under my skin that said trouble was coming. Deltas were a strange caste, one other dynamics didn't understand. We also had a sixth sense for violence, could almost taste it in the air, and as we raced along the corridor, I sensed it coming at us from all sides.

"*Next left, no, fuck it, go right!*"

"What the fuck is happening?" I snarled into the communicator.

"*You don't want to know,*" he said ominously. "*You're going to take the next left and wait at the end for me to give you the go. Third door on the left is going to be open. When I say go, you need to move past it fast.*"

"Jesus fucking Christ," I muttered. "Tell me this is the best route?"

"*It's the best I've got,*" the Gecko said, and for once, there was not a bit of humor in his voice.

"Are you going to get us out of this?"

"*Yes,*" he said. "*Just move fast and don't let her see what's going on in there. I'm not fucking squeamish, but it's giving me the creeps. Other direction, they're shooting shit up. Another group is now approaching from behind. You have to move forward.*"

We came to a stop at the end of this corridor as instructed. I could hear screams coming from ahead, the high-pitched kind I associated with torture.

"Sup?" Kade demanded.

"We got raiders approaching from behind, trouble right, and the only option we have is left. But left isn't good either."

Abby heaved her breath.

"Fuck," Kade muttered.

"We're gonna walk fast but also quietly. They're busy, so

they might not even notice. But if they do, we're going to fucking run. There are going to be sounds and shit going on in a room on the left. It's nothing to do with us, and we don't have the weapons or numbers to help, so we're not going to die trying, understood?"

Abby nodded, shaking so hard, her teeth were chattering, and that put me in a murderous mood.

"Got it," Kade said.

"Let's go," I said.

We set a brisk pace, footsteps quiet against the springy floor. The screams coming from the room died out to groans, whimpers, and quiet sobbing that set my teeth on edge. I could hear the ragged sound of Abby's breathing that had nothing to do with exertion and everything to do with fear.

Just as we closed in on the open door, another sharp, visceral scream pierced the air, and raucous laughter followed.

I looked, I didn't need to, knew I shouldn't, but I did. They had some poor bastard strung up, and a raider was peeling the captive's skin. A row of personnel in white lab coats sat huddled against the opposite wall.

"Help us!" one of the white coated civilians screamed.

The raider doing the peeling threw a look over his shoulder directly at us, and death entered his eyes.

"Oh god," Abby gasped as bullets tore into the wall behind us. Kade fisted her arm and half carried her down the corridor.

I went to go right at the end.

"*Left!!!*"

We turned left and ran.

"*It's clear ahead. Take the next right, and then ahead are double doors. The drop door mechanism will be on the inside.*"

We raced through the double doors into an agriculture pod. A rack of plants had been overturned near the door and pots and soil were strewn across the floor. Whoever had been here had beat a hasty retreat. "We're in," I said.

"It won't lock," Abby said, a frantic edge to her voice as she palmed the big red button with the words 'Emergency only' on a neat white plate above where a plastic cover had been flipped up. The red button was electronic, it wasn't like it needed force. "Why won't it shut? Oh god! It won't drop! That's why it's not already down."

Kade joined her, slamming his palm against the button several times. "Damn it!"

"We need some help here," I said into my communicator. The sound of automatic weapons was drawing closer, getting louder.

"*I've got nothing,*" the Gecko said. "*You have to do that from your end.*"

"What do you mean you can't help? What the fuck kind of hacker are you?"

"Yo! Whatsup?" Kade demanded. "Tell him to lock the fucking door."

"*There's going to be a mechanism somewhere. The panel to the right maybe. I got the cameras, that's as far as my control goes.*"

"The panel." I nodded to Kade. "Rip it off. See what's underneath."

Kade backed up and slammed the heel of his boot against the plate.

"Other exits?" I demanded of the hacker as Kade continued to kick out the plate.

"*No, they're spreading everywhere. You're not getting out without a fight. Maybe you'll be lucky, and they won't try the door.*"

The plate had buckled.

The automatic fire was getting closer.

"Are we going to be lucky?" I asked as I frantically looked around for something to brace the door.

"*No,*" was the Gecko's terse reply, just as shots bounced off the other side of the door.

"Fuck, Fuck, Fuck!" Kade muttered, finally getting his knife under the edge of the cover to leaver it up.

"Just shoot it," Abby hissed.

"Shoot what?" Kade said.

"Shoot the lock, the door. Shoot everything! I don't want to die!"

"*A mob is incoming. A dozen or so, all heavily armed.*"

Mumbling about bossy females, Kade shot out the plate. It pinged, sparks flew, and the cover clattered to the floor.

As Kade joggled the connector, I grabbed the nearest metal rack full of plants and pots and shoved them against the doors. "Hurry up with the fucking lock!"

I braced the rack against the barricade just as the mob hit the door. It shook the rack and nearly bowled me over. I planted my feet and pushed. Abby threw her smaller weight at it with me.

Cries, hoots, and random gunfire came from the other side. Fuck, they were high as a kite.

"It's not going to hold," Abby said as the next thud nearly flung us both off.

"Kade, the fucking door!"

"I'm trying!"

The pounding on the door continued. My feet were slipping. I couldn't hold it indefinitely.

"Get back, Abby. They're going to pop it."

"No!"

Fucking defiant woman!

All the sprinklers came on, and water rained down.

"What the actual fuck?!" I glared at Kade, boots slipping in the wet soil scattered over the floor.

The next big push from the raiders sent Abby flying to her hands and knees. I barely slammed it back.

The next shove, I lost footing, and the rack crashed to the floor.

"Got it," Kade roared.

The drop door slammed down.

Silence followed, broken only by the patter as water rained down from the sprinklers.

"That was close," the voice on my communicator said.

I heaved a breath, searching for Abby and finding her still on her knees, blinking at me, shaking up a storm.

"It's over," I said, approaching her slowly. I crouched beside her and carefully pushed back her wet hair from her forehead. "You okay?"

A heavy sob erupted from her chest, and she flung herself at me.

Fuck! I was an emotional void and didn't have a clue what the fuck to do. She clung, small hands fisting my shirt.

Her misery found a place inside me that I'd thought to be dead. I swallowed and shared a look with Kade before tapping my communicator. "Tell me there are no more entry points about to surprise us?"

"None. I lost the camera to the room when you shot out the drop door, but trust me that you hit it just in time. Military is incoming. Just hang tight. I'm going to update Lucian."

Chapter Three

Abby

Safe, we were finally safe, but I still couldn't make myself let go of a man who was a stranger to me. I was numb, and the only thing I could feel was his heart beating under my cheek. It offered comfort, as did the solid power of his body. I'd never looked my own death in the eye before, and it was fair to say I was shaken.

The sprinklers were still dousing us, not that I cared. I lacked the mental bandwidth to process what had just gone down, and despite the fact that I needed to find some self-control, I couldn't let Jordan go. The way his arms formed a band around me said he didn't mind.

Footsteps approached, crunching over soil and broken pots, and I dragged my nose from where it was buried against Jordan's chest to look back over my shoulder at Kade. He was so handsome, so *huge*. I'd been around alphas before, understood they had a magnetism that enchanted dynamics of every kind, yet these two were off the charts.

He closed the distance, stepping right up to me and putting his hand against the back of my neck. I heaved a breath in, my stomach performing a tumble, feeling a little woozy from the closeness and being between these two powerful males. I'd never envied omegas, but today, I was curious about what it was like to scent the pheromones and feel the inevitable pull.

They didn't need any help. Low in my belly came the tell-tale tightening and the sweet ache of sexual tension. It hardly seemed fair to the rest of society to bestow so much raw appeal upon these two individuals.

Gammas didn't produce pheromones, nor could we detect them, but our awareness of other's emotional states was excep-tional—it was one of the reasons I'd taken up a career that involved therapy.

It also had its downside. I could pick up on negative as well as positive emotions in others. Much like an empath omega might, I was acutely aware of them as both men and alphas, and how the air hummed with an awareness that went beyond ordi-nary human understanding.

Kade's fingers tightened briefly. "I'll see if I can shut these sprinklers off," he said, his body throwing off heat that I just wanted to arch up into.

His hand slipped away, and he backed up, leaving me instantly cold.

Jordan released me and, cupping my cheek, tipped my chin up until I met his eyes.

The sprinkler stopped abruptly, and I shivered, but not from the chill. No, it was from the emotions burning in Jordan's cool gray eyes.

Violence and proximity to death had an aphrodisiac effect on humans of every kind, but I thought it might be particularly potent in alphas and the reason the darkest of them were given controller ranks with omegas under their care. They were entrusted to protect them, a task rooted in their psyche, but they were also given leave, encouraged, and even expected to fuck the omegas under their care.

Investment, they called it—just a fancy word for submission someone had come up with to make it more politically palatable.

The general population outside the military knew nothing of how the relationship between alphas and omegas worked. I'd signed an NDA after I'd been approved to provide therapy services. Gammas were the preferred choice because we were naturally attuned to the alpha dynamic but didn't trigger them the way an omega would. Most alphas thought of gammas as defective omegas. We experienced no heat, had no alluring scent, and couldn't take a knot any better than any other non-omega dynamic.

My interest had always been purely professional in the alphas I'd met. So what was different about this? Perhaps the violence had pushed Jordan and Kade over the line, for I sensed only a thin membrane held all their natural aggression and dominance in check. As Jordan stared down at me, I understood that he wanted me with a hunger he was fighting to contain.

I'd never been with an alpha before, not that I'd lived a wild existence with any dynamic, but I'd had a few brief relationships with beta males. Not one of them had lit me up like this.

Jordan's eyes lowered to my lips. "You're trembling," he said in that low, slightly roughened voice.

"I'm just cold," I said, stepping back and breaking the spell, because I might do something stupid otherwise. I looked much like an omega, and in the circumstances, perhaps they viewed me as a good second best.

I didn't aspire to be an omega, nor did I desire to be anyone's second choice...even as appealing as they both were.

It felt safer to lower my lashes, to hide my eyes and the window into my erotic thoughts. After signing the NDA, I'd learned all about the secret side of control, about how they only allocated controller status to the darkest, most dominant males, using omegas as a means of tempering alpha aggression.

"Good news," Jordan said abruptly, stirring me from my thoughts. "Military just turned up. Looks like the raiders are fleeing."

"Why am I waiting for a catch?" Kade asked.

Jordan shrugged. "Yeah, looks like we're going to be here for a while."

"How long?" Kade asked. I didn't miss the hot glance he sent my way before he turned back to Jordan.

I moved farther away, trying to gain control of this strange compulsion sweeping through me.

"They're hooking an umbilical cord up near the docks. According to the station diagnostics, there is infrastructure damage blocking the path to us. They need heavy-duty cutting equipment, and they're going to have to ship it in."

"Fuck, that's going to take them hours," Kade said, frowning. "Abby's soaked, and it's not exactly warm in here."

I turned away. I couldn't handle their concern. I might break down into a blubbering wreck.

"Good girl," Jordan had said approvingly when he explained the dangers to me. Why did I even care about his validation? Why did I want him to call me a good girl again?

If I were an omega, they wouldn't allow me space. They would be holding me close, purring for me, not giving me quarter, because their instincts would be clamoring to offer me the comfort I needed, especially two alphas who were obviously controllers. Despite the inequality that was an omega's lot, there was a certain allure to being controlled.

I sent a speculative look their way. They stood a few paces

away, heads close together and talking too softly for me to hear. They were beautiful, sexually appealing men, muscular, supremely fit, and capable...*very* capable. I imagined the feel of their big hands skimming over my body would be glorious, then their lips...and their cocks. Everyone knew about an alpha's cock.

I fidgeted with my wet dress, which was clinging to me like a second skin. My curves drew attention, the kind that weak men took as a green light. I didn't even mind people looking. I wasn't immune to the image of the hot alphas who came through my door. Still, I drew the line at persistent, unwanted advances and had taken to wearing clothes that hid everything because it was easier.

I tried to pull the wet material from my body, but it sucked straight back to my skin the moment I let go. *Great!* My nipples were rock hard from the cold and sticking out. I might as well have painted a target on my breasts.

Distracted, I hadn't realized I was huffing and muttering under my breath until both their heads swung my way, and just like that, the tension cranked up another notch.

I could have turned away or hunched my shoulders, but I'd be lying to myself if I said their attention was unwelcome.

My nipples peaked painfully hard, and I straightened a little, presenting myself. I might have had a poor sense of smell, but theirs would be exceptional, and my wayward thoughts were being revealed through my body's response.

I became perfectly still, and despite my conscience screaming not to complicate my life, I couldn't turn away. The air thickened further, making me a little dizzy.

Maybe I couldn't smell their pheromones but they still somehow affected me?

They looked toward each other. Long seconds passed, and then as if by silent cue, they moved.

"I'll go check," Jordan said. He walked past me toward the drop door.

What he was checking, I had no idea. I was too focused on Kade's built body as he stepped up before me. "How are you, Abby?"

His presence had been intense enough while I was distracted by the fight to survive. Now that we were safe, it was all-consuming.

"I'm good," I said, although I was soaking wet, shaking, and more aroused than I'd been in my life. *Good* didn't come close to describing my mental state.

His gaze roamed the length of my body before returning to meet my eyes. He winked. "I've been trying not to notice how hot you are, but it's a lot harder now you're all wet. I'd offer you my T-shirt, but it's also wet."

I blushed. I never blushed—ever. I was a no-nonsense therapist and used to dealing with dynamics of all kinds.

"You're not shy about giving instructions in the heat of battle," he continued. "You look all sweet omega but with a hidden badass side. I like it."

I'd borne witness to more than a few feisty omegas during my time as a therapist, so I wondered where the notion of them being sweet came from, but I did appreciate his praise.

My meandering thought process came to an abrupt stop.

Wait...did he think I was an omega?

"I'm not—Ah, I'm not an omega," I said, feeling suddenly awkward.

He grinned. "I know that. You're a dynamic, though, aren't you?" His eyes held mine. "A gamma, at a guess?"

I swallowed. Not once in my life had anyone, dynamic or non-dynamic, correctly identified my caste. Most presumed I was a non-dynamic or a beta.

He stepped a fraction closer, sending little frissons of arousal pooling in my belly.

"I—Do you...ahh." What I was trying to say? Was I about to offer to invest, aka submit? What the hell was wrong with me? I was about to make a fool of myself. I wasn't an omega. He knew I wasn't an omega. I shouldn't even know what investment meant!

I knew more about the alpha dynamic than most alphas knew about themselves. Etiquette dictated I explain to him I was a therapist who worked with alphas and omegas and that I put a professional distance between us before this exploded out of control.

Parts of that secret world of alpha control had given rise to a swathe of dark fantasies. I definitely liked the thought of submitting, of giving myself over to a dominant man, an alpha, and his power, of him doing anything he chose because I'd given my permission...given him absolute control.

I was a gamma, I was supposed to covet deltas, but there were no deltas here, only two alphas who sparked my interest in a way no alpha ever had before. Alphas could read an omega and instinctively gave him or her what they needed, no matter how extreme or dark that might seem to an outsider. Except I wasn't an omega, and although alphas might find relationships with betas and other dynamics, it would always be a second best.

Or would it?

A tremble rippled through my body. Anticipation? Kade wanted me to scratch an itch. The post battle hormones were riding him just as they were riding me.

"What?" he demanded. He was young, they both were. Kade, in particular, might be even younger than me, yet when he spoke, it carried all the weight of an alpha at ease with himself and his place in the world.

Common sense finally prevailed before I bit off more than I could handle. "It's nothing. I'm being...foolish." It was the pressure and the stress messing with my natural calm. He was a fit, virile alpha in his prime and sinfully handsome, but heaven help me, for once, I wished I were an omega and that I could give myself over to Kade's control.

Either of their control...or both.

Yes, I liked the sound of both.

God, what the hell was wrong with me? What had I been thinking to consider offering submission to them? They would most likely laugh!

"Still waiting for you to explain, Abby."

I risked a glance up, but the moment I did, I felt the heat of another presence behind me. Kade was staring over my shoulder at Jordan, and something silent passed between them. I tried to turn, but Kade caught my chin, turning my face back to him. "Uh-uh, sweetheart. Eyes on me. Tell me what you were going to say."

Warmth blanketed me from their bodies, reminding me of how chilled I was. The words stuck in my throat. I tried desperately to think of something else to say, but my mind offered me nothing. Further, my spiraling libido demanded that I say exactly what I'd intended to, consequence be damned.

"I...was going to offer to—" I couldn't get the word out.

"You were going to offer to invest," he said, blue eyes darkening. My gasp told him all he needed to know.

"It was ridiculous...and there are two of you. I shouldn't even know...what it means," I finished lamely, cursing my rambling mouth and feeling mortified.

Leaning down, he placed his lips close to my ear. "Offer your submission, Abby," he said.

I jumped as Jordan's hands settled over my hips. He, too, leaned down and said, "Offer it to both of us."

Arousal pooled in the pit of my stomach, and I shuddered.

"Submit, sweetheart," Kade said. "We know you want to. You might not be an omega, but we can still smell aroused. Give us your submission. We'll take care of the rest."

"Yes," I said, pushing words past the tightness in my throat. "I submit."

Chapter Four

Abby

I had done it, said the words, and something told me they were not the kind of words one could take back.

My mind went into some sort of shutdown mode where I had no capacity to think...only feel. I became hyper-aware of their presence and potent masculinity.

We were in a garden pod, surrounded by racks of vegetables and fruit...and soil. There was an awful lot of soil. We had just survived an attack and were trapped behind a sealed door, on the other side of which anything might be happening.

It felt wildly inappropriate to be even thinking about this.

"Just to be absolutely clear," Kade said, looking me straight in the eye. "When you said you were giving your submission, you mean you're giving yourself to us to do whatever we want with?"

I nodded slowly.

"Fucking," he said, making my eyes widen and bringing a little spasm to my womb. "We are going to want to fuck you."

Swallowing past the tightness in my throat, I nodded again.

"Say the words, Abby. I don't want there to be any confusion about what's about to happen and that you agree."

"Yes," I said.

"Both of us," he continued bluntly.

My heart gave a little thud of anticipation. "Yes," I said again.

Kade smiled. "Good girl... Now there's just a small detail we haven't covered yet—we're not alphas."

"Oh," I said inadequately, my brows pinching together in confusion. I'd been sure they had to be alphas. Beta controllers were being phased out, but I supposed there must be some in service. Or maybe they were former beta controllers. Still, his comment had thrown me off a little. They just seemed more... intense than I presumed a beta might be.

"Are you beta controllers?" I asked, searching myself to see if I was disappointed by this discovery. I thought I might have been, which was ridiculous because neither man was disappointing. They were the most imposing betas I'd ever met.

Clearly, I needed to seek therapy for myself, which was ironic, all things considered. Maybe it was because alphas were so close to deltas—my dynamic match. I'd never met a delta and likely never would, so I'd latched onto them as a second best, much like they were seeing me.

The smirk that bloomed on Kade's lips brought a clench to belly. He shook his head slowly. "No, we're deltas."

The blood drained from my face. I tried to take a step back, only to find the wall of Jordan's body. His hands tightened on my hips, and his dark chuckle stirred a frisson of fear.

Deltas? No, they were teasing me. It was a very poor joke. Deltas were rarer than omegas, and then there was the matter of their hook... No, I wasn't going there.

"Ah," Kade said. "I do love that look on a woman's face

when they realize we have a hook. And unlike alphas, we don't need to wait for a rut or bonding before it comes out to play. It's there all the time." He winked. "It does sting a little when it latches, so I've been told, but we'll make it good for you." His eyes turned hooded, predatory. "Make sure you're so thoroughly distracted, you'll barely notice it."

Jordan leaned in close again. "And once we're latched nice and deep, you won't stop fucking coming."

A cold shiver swept the length of my spine. What had I just done? What the hell had I agreed to do...with two deltas?

"You should have told me," I whispered, hardly able to comprehend the magnitude of their confession and what it would mean. I experienced a sudden epiphany as to where the hook would go—deep in my womb. I didn't care what Kade said about it only stinging a little. It was going to hurt no matter how they might try to distract me.

"Do you have any idea how many women run screaming when they find out you're a delta?" Kade asked.

"Most of them," Jordan replied before I had a chance to speak. "I could hardly believe our luck when you offered up your pussy like that. I've never been with a gamma before. Have you, Kade?"

Kade shook his head. "No, but I've heard they're very sensitive. We'll need to make sure she's very thoroughly aroused."

"Not a problem," Jordan said, his voice a deep rumble behind me. "I can't wait to taste her."

"Me neither," Kade murmured before his head lowered and his lips closed over mine.

The first touch was like an electric current passing through me—soft, yet firm, and oh so demanding. His mouth moved over mine, tasting with little sips that set my heart thudding and a tingling awareness shooting straight to my core. He consumed me, one drugging kiss at a time, distracting me from thoughts of what was to come next. I leaned into him, wanting more, my hands pressed to the hard wall of his chest and utterly unaware of anything beyond the two of us.

His big hands cupped my face with such gentle reverence that I might have been forgiven for forgetting that he was a delta about to do unspeakable things to my body because that was how their anatomy worked. Lifting his lips from mine, he whispered, "Open for me, sweetheart. Let me taste you."

My lips parted without hesitation. Fear became a distant memory the moment his tongue slipped past my lips to tangle with mine. A whimper escaped my throat. I'd gone from zero to wanting to beg, and all Kade had done was kiss me.

"My turn."

I'd forgotten that Jordan was there. How was that possible while his hands rested lightly over my hips?

Those hands skimmed up to my waist as Kade's lips slowly parted from mine. Then Jordan's hold tightened, and I looked down to where his hands spanned over my plain green dress. A languid heat rolled through me, seeing his hands against me... feeling them there. I drew a shaky breath in and tried to process what was happening.

I couldn't.

"Poor baby," Kade said, just as Jordan gripped a handful of my hair, tugged my head back, and closed his lips over mine.

Kade's kiss had been sweet. Jordan's kiss was like being dropped into a maelstrom—hungry, savage, and dominating my every sense. A moan rose up from the pit of my stomach, and his fingers tightened over my hair at the back of my neck, angling my head further while he continued to plunder my mouth.

I gave myself over to the heady sensations, and just as I thought I was at the limit of stimulation, two warm hands closed over my breasts.

"Fuck, these are nice tits," Kade said, his voice thick with need as he cupped me. He squeezed them together, just as Jordan plunged his tongue into my mouth. I moaned. "We need to get her out of these wet clothes."

Jordan tore his lips from mine, and his hold loosened on my hair. We were both breathing heavily. "Good idea," he said.

Chapter Five

Jordan

Her face had turned as white as a sheet at the mention of us being deltas. It wasn't until Kade took me aside a few minutes ago that it dawned on me what was eating me up, why the itch that sometimes burrowed under my skin had risen to a roar.

My body was in a state of riot, as being trapped with a gamma was every delta's wet dream. No way was she leaving this room without getting fucked.

Then the icing on the cake was Abby offering up her submission.

Deltas were every bit as dominant as an alpha, and in some ways, we were worse. Any male who got turned on by the thought of hooking into a woman's womb had to be fucked-up, right?

I'd nearly lost my load, and all I'd done was kiss her. No, that wasn't kissing, that was me trying to consume her body and soul. I'd heard other deltas talking about gammas, saying what a perfect fit they were for a delta's cock and hook.

I couldn't wait to get inside her. She'd be lucky if she could find the energy to stand by the time we were both done.

"I don't think—"

"Shut the fuck up," I rumbled next to her ear. No way was I taking any bullshit from her about changing her mind. "Keep talking, baby, and I'll find something big to plug your mouth with."

Her tiny body trembled against mine. I kept a tight fist on her hair, tugging it just a little to remind her to behave.

She whimpered, and I looked down to watch where Kade had cupped her tits through the ugly green smock she wore. I couldn't wait to get her naked. I'd already had my hands on her enough to know some sweet curves were underneath.

"You offered yourself to us," Kade said, pinching her nipples through the material and making her squirm. "Asked us to fuck you, didn't you now?"

"Yes!"

"You change your mind, sweetheart?"

After about a second, during which I nearly lost my fucking mind, she said, "No."

"Good, because we all know it would've been a lie if you'd said otherwise."

Her shocked gasp went straight to my balls. Somehow I restrained myself from throwing her to the floor and rutting her like a savage. Alphas weren't the only dynamics who enjoyed taking a woman roughly, but they could keep their little omegas. I had my own prize in my hands.

"Glasses," I said, carefully slipping them from her face. I put them on a nearby plant rack before turning back to get my first proper look at her pretty eyes. "Don't want to get them broken."

"Let's get you out of these clothes, sweetheart," Kade said as he caught hold of the hem and drew it up.

"God, please!"

Her impatience lit an echoing feeling in me. I felt like I was on fucking fire. We stripped her, taking turns to swallow up her cries as we peeled her out of her dull dress, only to find pale lacy underwear that was enough to bring me to my knees.

"Fuck, I can't believe this was hiding underneath that dress," Kade murmured, taking his time unwrapping her.

She had gotten turned about during the process, and I finally got the reward of my hands on her naked tits, while Kade drew her panties over her beautifully rounded ass.

"Fuck, look how tiny her waist is," Kade muttered, and I smirked at how rough his voice sounded. He was hanging on to his sanity with a thread, but we both were. "Her ass is so fucking lush." He filled his big hands with her ass cheeks and squeezed them hard enough to turn the skin white around his fingers. "Like a perfect peach. Makes me want to take a bite. I want her ass first. You can have her pussy, but I want in this ass."

I growled softly, cupping her face in one hand and kissing her gasps up.

"Hush, baby," I said between kisses. "Let Kade have what he needs."

"I don't—" She gasped as I sucked a bite against her throat. "I've never—" I kissed up the next words.

"Ah, fuck." Kade groaned. "No one has had this ass, have they?"

I didn't know what he was doing to her, but she went wild in my arms, and I had to snake my arm around her waist to hold her still.

"How could someone not have taken this?" he asked as

though genuinely confused. "My dick's damn near embarrassing me with how badly he wants in here."

That stirred a chuckle from me. Kade wasn't well known for his restraint in anything, but especially when fucking. We did everything in twos, and contrary to popular opinion, women weren't always on board with a package deal and less so when they discovered what we were. They generally came in two flavors—the pain junkies, and the ones that ran for the hills, screaming.

But gammas, they were our match for a reason.

Abby

I was naked, while they were still fully clothed—something in this equation was very wrong.

It was all very wrong. They were deltas...with hooks...who were talking about taking my ass like it was a done deal.

It wasn't a done deal, and I'd tell them as much just as soon as I came up for air. Only that wasn't happening. One or other of them had occupied my mouth from the moment I'd submitted. This didn't come with an opt out clause. Omegas didn't get a choice to tap out with an alpha if it was getting too much, and I was getting the impression deltas were exactly the same.

How could I have missed what was so obvious now?

"Ummm!" Kade played with my pussy, sliding his finger through the slickness, before circling my clit over and over until I was panting into Jordan's mouth. Then he pushed two fingers deep, stretching me from behind, and all I could think about was whether he would follow through and slide them back and push them into my ass. I didn't want that, I really didn't. So why did the prospect arouse me so much?

Jordan finally lifted his head, and his big hand closed over the front of my throat. Eyes meeting mine, he gently squeezed. "Something you want to say?" he asked.

My mouth opened, but no sound came out. My lips were a little puffy and tingly from his kiss. I felt like I was drugged, under some kind of compulsion. God, there was something so wildly arousing about meeting one man's eyes while another was touching you intimately. They were an unnatural stormy gray, seeming to swirl without my glasses. His hair, I noticed, was tangled. A blush flooded my cheeks when I realized my hands had done that, drawing him closer as I demanded a deeper kiss.

Kade continued kissing up the back of my neck, making all the little hairs rise, causing me to groan. I'd wanted to say something. What, I had no idea anymore.

"We're gonna take good care of you," Jordan said.

I nodded slowly, aware on a distant level that we were in an agriculture pod on a space station that had just been subjected to a raid. Even now, somebody could be at the door, attempting to rectify whatever was broken after Kade had forced the security door to drop.

My lashes lowered to half-mast as Kade's hands skimmed up and cupped my breasts from behind. He tugged on my nipples, grinding his hard length into me and pushing me against Jordan. I felt so tiny between them, and vulnerable, caught under the spell of Jordan's heated stare, awash with sensation and emotions so thick, I could scarcely breathe.

They had just saved me. In the primal part of my brain, I felt the act justified a reward. We lived in a civilized world, one stained by darker animalistic urges that had ripped through all dynamics, but in particular, the alphas and omegas. What I'd only just come to understand was that it applied to deltas and gammas as well.

The copper virus had changed ordinary people into something else. I'd often thought of myself as a very nonsexual being trapped in a very sexual body, but as I stared up into Jordan's stormy eyes, I recognized myself as unrealized matter waiting for somebody to awaken me.

I groaned again as Kade pinched my nipples with just a little bite, pulling on a thread that ran all the way down to my core. "I'm scared," I whispered, rubbing my thighs together restlessly.

Jordan's face instantly softened.

Kade stilled before his hands lowered to my waist, leaving my nipples throbbing and tingling. "You've got nothing to be scared about, baby."

The endearment rolled off his tongue with ease. He was a beautiful, built man, the kind that caused women's panties to spontaneously melt as they begged to be in my position.

Jordan's thumb brushed up under my chin, tipping toward him so he could meet my eyes. "You're not really scared, are you?"

I frowned. Was I scared? I ought to have been, but it had been more of an instinctual statement, a means of slowing the onslaught down because they were collectively overwhelming me.

"We will never do more than you can take," Jordan said.

"Ever," Kade agreed, then his lips lowered to my throat and trailed featherlight kisses over the skin to my shoulder.

I shivered. It was cold here, but I was burning hot.

"Can you trust us?" Jordan asked. "Can you let go of all those inhibitions that society places on you? Can you free yourself for us? Because I promise you, if you can, we will blow your fucking mind."

Kade's lips were performing magic against the side of my throat. His hands were on my waist, the touch light, yet I was more aroused by his subtle stimulation than every other lover I'd had in the height of passion.

"Once an omega submits, that's it—game over," Jordan said.

I nodded slowly. God, I just wanted them to put their hands on me intimately again. Why had I slowed this down?

That was right—they were deltas. They came with a hook.

"I don't think I can take it." I shook my head, trying to clear it. "I've only ever been with a beta."

Jordan's nostrils flared, and Kade sucked hard against my throat.

I groaned.

"You're a gamma," Jordan said. "Genetically designed for us and only us."

Kade lifted his head, and Jordan's fingers lowered to collar my throat, tightening just enough to make me aware of him, his power, and his control. Panic bloomed as his fingers sank deeper oh so slowly, his hand so huge, it completely surrounded me until there was no breath for a brief moment. My hand shot up, closing over his wrist, only I made no move to wrench his hand free.

I'd been so focused on the lack of air that I hadn't registered how Kade's hand was moving, skimming down over my belly, between my thighs, until two thick fingers plunged into my dripping core. Jordan's fingers tightened again, but more a promise that brought a heightened awareness.

Heat spiraled inside me as Kade began to work his fingers in and out, those wet, sticky sounds like a loud speaker announcing my state of arousal.

"I think she likes that," Kade said.

"I think so too," Jordan agreed, his eyes focused on my lips.

Even the way they were discussing me while they were both touching me, pleasuring me, to be the subject of their intense focus, further compounded my intoxication with them.

Jordan squeezed lightly, and I opened my mouth on a silent gasp. Panic danced on my periphery as he closed his mouth over mine, trapping the air in my lungs. The darkly erotic act sent me spinning as Kade's busy fingers thrust in and out, making me tingle and woozy with lust. They centered their touch upon me, and the room and events past faded from my mind. Jordan swallowed up my breathless pants, while Kade made my pussy ache so sweetly.

My nails scored Jordan's wrist. He didn't mind it, nor did they stop their sensual assault. Then he dragged his lips from mine, breath heavy as he held my eyes as I panted and twitched and felt heat fill my cheeks. I was so close and yet so very vulnerable here, naked, between two men I barely knew. Heaven help me, how they knew me and my body, and how easily they played me...

"Come for me. Come for Kade. I want your cum running all over his hand."

Then he squeezed again, cupping my cheek with his other hand and holding my gaze as my gasps became more pronounced, while Kade, fingers buried deep, worked his thumb back and forth over my swollen clit. I blinked, wanting to escape the intensity of Jordan's gaze, even as my body splintered into a climax. The spasms were not done with me when he closed his mouth over mine, kissing up my groans, tongue plundering every contour of my mouth.

Kade's thick fingers took the full force of my gripping inner channel. "Good girl," Kade said. The twitches of pleasure turned to cringing at the sensitivity, but I was pinned squarely between them and there was no escaping this.

All three of us were breathing heavy in the wake. Kade remained buried intimately inside me as Jordan backed up enough for his eyes to roam over me.

"Fuck, you look so hot, panting, tits quivering," Jordan said.

"Didn't know women like this were real. Off the fucking charts." He reached down and pulled Kade's fingers from inside me.

My breath hitched as he lifted Kade's sticky fingers to his mouth and sucked them clean. His eyes rolled back, and he growled deep in his chest.

I swear I had another mini climax just watching the pleasure on his face.

He released Kade's fingers. "Fuck, I need to take the edge off," Jordan said. "I won't last long enough to get my hook in otherwise."

Kade's chuckle was dark. "On your knees, sweetheart," he said. As Jordan reached for the buckle of his pants, Kade closed his hand over my nape and gently pushed.

I glanced over my shoulder, finding myself the object of his dark gaze.

"Down you go."

I fell to my knees, throat aching a little, aware of the soreness where Kade had sucked love bites and the blood pounding in my clit and pussy. Scattered soil and plants offered a cushion of sorts for my knees, while in front of me stood a hulking delta male, muttering curses as he worked his zipper down and shucked his pants past his hips. His cock bobbed free, thick, long, ruddy, with a strangely bulbous head.

I swallowed and glanced up at him through my lashes. He smirked and brushed the hair back from my cheek. "Open up," he said, and stepping forward, took his cock in his other hand and presented it to me.

I opened my mouth. There was no thought to deny him. I'd just had the best orgasm of my life, was still throbbing, and desperately wanted more, but specifically, I wanted his cock, to taste him, to feel him inside me in any way I could. I swirled my tongue around the tip, lapping up the salty essence before he pushed deep, then I gagged. He pulled almost out and stared down at where my mouth was stretched around the fat cockhead.

"Looks like we've got our work cut out," Kade said. Distantly, I heard the faint rustle of him undressing behind me, but all I could see, feel, and taste was before me as Jordan drove his cock in and out of my mouth, filling me, stretching me. He took me roughly, grunting in satisfaction, eyes hooded with pleasure.

I hummed around him, pussy soaked, desperate to please him as they had pleased me. My fingers wrapped around the base of his hot shaft, now sticky from my lips. I cupped his balls with my other hand, and he rewarded me with another growl.

God, I could listen to that sound all day, and I was determined to make him growl again. I may be on my knees, but I'd never felt more powerful.

I took over, bobbing my head up and down, trying to relax my jaw and take him deeper, making myself gag this time.

"Fuck, she's enthusiastic," Kade said gruffly. His hands were on the back of my neck, now guiding me up and down Jordan's cock, and somehow, that made the moment even more intimate, being between them, having both of them touching me, especially while I was doing this.

"She's a gamma," Jordan replied, as if this were the answer to everything.

I didn't know what that meant. I had always felt alone, never quite fitting in with the rest of the world yet not minding that either, but for once, I felt the center of something much larger than me.

"Did you know they're together?" Jenna had said while we'd been waiting to disembark the fateful transport, which had led me to the here and now. *"Deltas share everything, including each other and their chosen gamma."*

51

Now, enlightenment dawned, and I could well believe it. The way Jordan had casually taken Kade's fingers and licked them clean, done so naturally... They were men who were intimate with one another, and I was assaulted by curiosity for how it might be when two powerful males, both unquestionably dominant, pleasured each other.

Behind me, Kade sank to his knees, his big body blanketing mine with heat, making me shiver and suck lovingly on Jordan's cock with renewed enthusiasm.

"Fuck I'm going to come," Jordan rumbled.

"Not yet," Kade said. "I need inside her while she's sucking you off. Fuck, if this isn't the hottest thing I've ever seen, her mouth straining to wrap around you. Does it feel good?"

"It feels fucking amazing," Jordan said, breath a grunt. "Hot and clenching when she gags around me."

Kade's hands were on my hips, lifting my ass, his cock thick and hot, grinding into my flesh. My focus split three ways—Jordan before me, Kade behind me, and wondering how it would look if Kade were to take Jordan's cock. My stomach clenched with unmistakable interest. I thought he would take it easier than me, and if, as Jenna implied, they were together, then he would probably be accomplished... I might even learn from him. It was hard to process such a male worshiping another, like such submissive roles were reserved for lesser dynamics. Only submission wasn't weakness, was it? No, submission was power. How had I never understood this before?

I'd never gotten on my knees, not once in my life, never prayed to a male of any kind, until today.

"Brace yourself, Abby," Kade said. "This is gonna get a little rough."

Jordan growled lowly, and I thought it held approval.

Despite Kade's warning, nothing could have prepared me

to be taken simultaneously by two men, which wasn't even a fantasy for me. I hadn't been convinced I could handle more than one, and I still wasn't.

I wanted to protest, and was sure my eyes were a little wild, but Jordan cupped my cheeks and kept me there, pinned, lips stretched around his cock. My nostrils flared as I became aware of being trapped in such an intimate way as Kade snaked his arm around my waist to hold me still and drove deep in a single, brutal thrust.

I groaned and arched up, instinctively sucking, needing something to distract me from the pervasive fullness. Kade tightened his grip, holding still, letting me get used to him, although heaven, I thought neither time nor training would deliver results in this regard. The term *savage invasion* came to mind. I felt utterly possessed. Every nerve the length of my slick pussy woke up and paid attention in the most arresting way. My eyelids fluttered closed, and I lapped at Jordan's cock, trying to show him that I needed more of him as a distraction before I came undone.

"Fuck! She's gripping my cock so hard," Kade said gruffly. "Loosen up, sweetheart. Let me get inside."

Inside? I couldn't process what he meant by inside, not while Jordan began to thrust steadily, the surge and retreat, the gulped breaths when he wasn't plugging my throat snatching my focus from the thick club wedged like a tree trunk in my pussy.

I hadn't seen Kade's cock, couldn't bring myself to contemplate his size now it was inside, filling me so good. But there was more? He'd said I must relax so that he could get in.

In where?

Everything became hot as he moved in slow, shallow thrusts that pushed and pulled me on and off Jordan's cock. My mind might not have known what to make of this, but my body was all in. Sensitive nerves along my channel fired under the stimulation of hot male flesh, stretching me just right.

"Fuck," Jordan muttered, thrusting shallowly. My jaw, aching from holding him inside my mouth, was now on fire as I took him deeper. "I'm close to fucking coming already, she's sucking me so good."

"Come then," Kade said. "Fill her up. It's what she needs."

I blinked bleary eyes open to meet Jordan's dark gaze, taking in his expression, the raw lust, feeling it fan the fire inside me. Saliva and pre-cum leaked over my chin, my short damp hair sticking to my flushed cheeks. I felt like a mess—the most glorious, dirty, sexy mess.

As if my gaze was a trigger, Jordan grunted as he came down my throat, while Kade's fingers became immovable bands, keeping me still and locked on his cock. My nails dug into Jordan's thighs as hot ropey cum poured down my throat. I swallowed and coughed. When he didn't pull out, my eyes began to water.

I couldn't breathe.

The excess trickled out of my mouth, down my chin, and dripped onto my chest as my vision turned into sparkling dots, my heart racing and body surging. I was sure I was about to come...but I didn't, then Jordan's cock finally popped free.

Kade's hand was on my chin, turning me to face him. "Hot as fuck," he said as he swiped his thumb over my chin before pushing it between my parted lips. I sucked the sticky offering up, watching his blurry blue eyes darken before he planted his mouth over mine for a hot, wet kiss. I groaned, swaying against him, wrapped up in his embrace and aware of his cock, deep and intimate, flexing.

Jordan sank to his knees before me, claiming my mouth the moment Kade came up for air, and that fast, I was caught in a wildness again, pulling me deeper down into a sensual abyss.

Either one of them was enough, but together, they were a dark, depraved, and frightening kind of addictive.

I'd never needed nor coveted approval, but I felt theirs in the deep, grumbling growls, in the way their hands roamed over my body, the faint tremble telling me this meant as much to them as it did to me.

I'd never felt special nor comfortable with how a gamma fit into the larger dynamic world, and I definitely wasn't comfortable with my body. I made a point of hiding my curves because I didn't like attention, but for once, I basked in the heady glow of their approval.

"I need to do her rough," Kade said thickly.

Jordan hummed, capturing my face in his big hands, and oh how I was trapped by that look. "Good girl, you can take it."

Kade pulled out and immediately slammed back, going deeper, filling me further, forcing me open, and reminding me that there was indeed more. My lips popped open, and Jordan swallowed up my cry.

"Fuck, she feels so good wrapped around me," Kade said, grunting as he began to power into me. Each thrust juddered through my whole body, making a filthy, wet *slap* as our flesh met.

"Yeah?" Jordan said. "She sounds slick. I can't wait to have my turn."

The way they discussed me, their seamless ease with each other, and in sharing me... I couldn't imagine alphas doing this. I couldn't imagine many dominant males doing this, or even less dominant ones. It was hot, unbelievably hot, and I just let myself fall into their hands, let them take me away, trusted them, men I barely knew, because they made trusting them so easy when they played me this way, lifted me without effort toward a climax I sensed would break me for all other men.

Kade shifted his grip to my hips and began to piston in and

out with rough thrusts from which there was no escape. Our bodies slapped together fast and furiously, and my arousal went from hot to boiling in a matter of seconds.

I was going to come again, could feel it building higher and higher, and it was going to be cataclysmic.

Then the fat head of Kade's monstrous cock began to batter the entrance to my womb. Dark sensations rushed through me, and sweat popped out across my skin. It should have hurt, but instead, felt good in a twisted kind of way.

As I panted, Jordan kept his eyes locked on mine, watching the torment play out. "She can take it," he said, his gray eyes almost black.

I tried to shake my head because I didn't think I could take it, only I was held fast, and I wasn't being given a choice.

"We'll never give you more than you can handle," Jordan had said, but how would they know? How could they possibly understand my limits when I didn't know for myself?

Kade began adjusting the angle of every thrust until... *Oh god!* Every deep penetration connected perfectly with a spot inside that had me seeing stars for all the right reasons. A sweet achy sensation rose and rose, morphing, churning, grasping me, pulling me, *demanding.* I was going to come, and no sooner did I realize this then it ripped through me, setting me convulsing around his thick, hard length. *Oh god, oh god, oh god!*

"Good girl, that's it," Jordan said, "Come all over his cock. Fuck, that feels so good, doesn't it? Kade taking you deeply like you were meant to be, ruining your hot cunt."

His filthy, blunt words were further gasoline on my raging fire. I couldn't stop coming, and Kade slammed into me even harder. It didn't seem to matter what he did, my body was on fire for him. Jordan's hand skimmed down, his fingers seeking and finding my slippery, sensitive clit, where he strummed without mercy.

I understood what was coming, the rapturous cloud lifting from my mind as I acknowledged what came next.

"Take it," Jordan said, voice a low husky command. "Take it all."

Kade was going to hook me.

A squeal tore from my lips. Their responding growl was one of ruthless determination. Deep inside, something let go. Maybe I was broken? I couldn't find the capacity to care. I was too busy soaring high, contracting around him in the most intense climax of my life. Disconnected, I existed on another plane. Heat bloomed across the surface of my skin, sweat popped from my pores, and every hair follicle on my body came alive to pleasure. My nipples peaked to hardened points and tingled with the same erotic joy in an echo of the quaking in my womb. It was like we were joined everywhere, and I felt a perfect fullness—so, so full. My heart pounded and my pussy fluttered wildly as the climax refused to let me go.

I shivered, clinging to Jordan.

"Fuck," Jordan muttered. "Fuck, she's really taking your hook."

Kade grunted, and heat flooded inside me, his cock flexing as another savage climactic round of pleasure tore through my womb.

Kade

I was out of my fucking mind as Abby's perfect pussy locked down and milked every drop of cum. I cupped her face and angled my mouth over hers in a breathtaking kiss, my cock flexing and dumping a ton of fucking cum right where it needed to be

Her hot cunt continued to clench enthusiastically around me. Little gamma was greedy for it, so it seemed only fair that I should spoil her. My woman would be leaking cum for a week at this rate, because I kept on coming. I was damp, sticky, covered in soil, and cum was dripping down my balls. My heart was pounding in my ribs, and I swear every drop of blood was trying to cram into my dick...and still, she kept on twitching over the head of my cock, coaxing me to give her even more. I tried, balls aching and straining to find the last reserves. My only disappointment was not getting to play with her ass, but I figured we needed something better than wet soil under her when I went for that.

"Fuck, I need her again," Jordan muttered. His fingers were still busy between her thighs, catching the root of my cock and balls as he slid his big fingers back and forth—little wonder neither of us were coming down.

A panted chuckle escaped my throat, because this was fucking insane. I continued to rock, tugging lightly at where my hook was buried in her womb, and with each little tug, another tiny jet of cum spurted out.

"Fuck, look at her stomach," Jordan muttered, leaning back and splaying a big hand over her belly. "She's all swollen up."

"Don't," I pushed through gritted teeth. Too late, I glanced down over her. Fuck, he was right. I had filled her all up, couldn't remember coming this long and hard.

"Please..." She groaned, twitching. "God, please, no more."

Poor baby was at her limit and growing restless. Unfortunately, I was high on pleasure and my hook was having none of my instructions to calm the fuck down.

"Settle yourself, baby," I said, "or it's going to take forever for my hook to let you go."

Chapter Six

The viral program was based on Tolis for three years. During this time, we increased beta, delta, and gamma dynamics threefold, but yields of other dynamics had been low. Betas were the natural follower dynamic. Deltas were aggressive and territorial, like alphas, but differed in specific physiological characteristics. While gammas shared many psychological characteristics with an omega, they didn't experience heat and were unaffected by pheromones.

What the government wanted were more omegas, but the program on Tolis had yielded few.

The program director, Erison Tsing, believed the work a spectacular failure.

I thought otherwise. It allowed me to meet the rarest dynamic of them all—the gamma.

These quiet, often studious dynamics were universally intelligent. Surprisingly, given their highly divergent personalities, they were often born to theta parents. Rather than the pursuit of prestige I'd witnessed in thetas, gammas were drawn toward humanitarian and impact pursuits, often becoming doctors, counselors, and tireless aid workers.

The anatomical differences in the delta-gamma dynamic match led to some difficulties in the bonding process, which were overcome only by time or a restraining order.

While alphas were known for being territorial toward omegas under their care, deltas were exponentially more so when it came to gammas. One might conclude that this primitive, and unhealthy idea of ownership over what they viewed as compatible breeding stock was a result of them being incredibly rare.

While I believed that was part of it, I also concluded, through a combination of direct and anecdotal interviews, that it was simply a deeply embedded imperative of the delta dynamic, heightened by the males forming a 'pack,' usually of two, but occasionally three males.

Restraining orders were ineffective and were more to give the gamma time to adjust. Deltas were relentless, determined, and inventive in their quest to claim a mate and suffered no qualms about breaking rules, laws, or people who stood in their way.

Once both males 'hooked' the gamma, a psychic connection was established. Much like an alpha-omega bond, subsequent attempts at separation were catastrophic. Knowing they had a get out of jail pass once bonded led to extreme risk-taking in pursuing their chosen mate.

While I thought a lot of alphas and omegas to be a challenge of the highest order, what happened between deltas and gammas was a different level of barbaric.

∼ Doctor Lillian Brach

Abby

After the attack on Kix29, I'd been put on a fast transport straight to a military base on Tolis. It was a relief to find myself on solid ground. With the added bonus of thousands of troops and a state-of-the-art defense, it offered a sense of safety while I processed the events.

As a therapist, I understood that I now carried scars, not just from confronting my own mortality but from meeting deltas for the first time in my life.

Wild was the word that came to mind whenever I recalled the encounter. The things they had done to me defied logic and the boundaries of human physical capabilities. Despite how improbable my taking a hook was, I was not damaged in any way, albeit being a little sore immediately afterward.

I was a gamma, so perhaps this was natural.

Hopefully, I would have some answers after I met with the famous Doctor Lillian Brach, a high-ranking consultant on the viral program and daughter of a governor on the Empire's ruling council. Her office was in the viral research center, a tall, imposing building in the heart of the capital city. Unusually for someone in such an important position, Lilly was an omega, and despite her lofty status and upbringing, eschewed any honorific by insisting I call her Lilly.

In the media pictures, she looked beautiful...but they didn't do her justice. I'd never met an ugly omega, but Lilly was simply stunning, with golden blonde hair and big amber eyes. I'd acquired a few shapeless dresses several sizes too big since arriving at the base, and beside Lilly, I felt like a frumpy blob.

"Have you ever met Ryker?" I blurted out before I could help myself. She had just offered me a drink. Her smiling beta assistant by the name of Merry had only just closed the door, and we hadn't got past pleasantries.

Lilly shook her head. "No, I don't believe I have. Why do you ask?"

I wasn't one for uncensored slips, so goodness knew why I chose to now. "No reason," I said inadequately. "I had a therapy session with him this morning, that was all."

Ryker was an alpha who'd been on my books for several years and arguably my most complex client. Often, we performed sessions remotely, but he was on Tolis, so we'd met in person today, which was always a challenge. He had been reprimanded again for an infringement, but his response was playful and lacking in remorse. He ticked many boxes on the psychopathy scale, but he was functional in his role as a soldier, other than his propensity for inappropriate use of weapons, particularly rocket-propelled grenade launchers, which proved terminal for infrastructure when in his hands.

Still, he was handsome, like media star level of handsome, and as much as I thought he would be the worst possible choice of mate for the beautiful and brilliant omega sitting opposite me on the lilac couch, they would look simply stunning together.

Lilly's expression said I was baffling her, although she smiled politely. "I don't meet very many alphas in my line of work. I've mostly worked with omegas, but we have several gammas here, and their needs are closely related. I make a point of meeting where schedules permit."

"Thank you," I said, banishing the image of Lilly and Ryker from my mind because that would not end well for anyone, but partially Lilly. Besides, Lilly was one of the few omegas working as a civilian and didn't even have an alpha mate, never mind a controller. I was confident they had only given Ryker controller status in an attempt to soften the worst of his personality traits. So far, it hadn't worked that I could tell.

"How much education have you had on your dynamic?" she asked, getting down to the matter.

"Very little," I admitted. "I never gave my dynamic status much attention. In many ways, I'm treated like a beta. I wasn't even curious about it...until recently." Now I was *extremely* curious. I could feel my cheeks heating, so I plowed straight on. "My parents are thetas, so my revealing as a gamma came as a shock to them. Supporting the military is very lucrative, and my parents encouraged the pathway for my career. Now that I have taken on this role, I find the work interesting and varied."

"Many gammas take on counseling roles of one kind or another," she said. "You might be surprised to learn you're often born to theta parents." She smiled. "Gammas have many similarities to omegas, in both stature and disposition, but have the benefit of neutrality in the dynamic lottery without the pheromone markers and heat cycles. You are largely free to pursue career choices at will."

"Largely?" I asked, feeling that prickling of unease, despite how positive the rest had sounded.

"Other than mating," she said, and I blanched. "I know the term is coarse to those outside the dynamic. I've canvassed for better education for gammas, as I believe it's warranted, given the unique nature of their bonding, but *mating* is the most accurate term for both alpha-omega and delta-gamma pairings."

"How does mating impact us?" I asked, feeling like I was about to tumble headfirst down a rabbit hole. I'd envisioned some light, unremarkable information sharing, but in less than five minutes, we were already discussing mating.

Her amber gaze held mine without flinching, yet I sensed her discomfort, although she hid it well.

"A psychic connection is formed during mating that is every bit as intense as that between an alpha and omega, and pregnancy likelihood is high. Afterward, you're tied to the delta pack for life. Separation is not advised, as it can prove catastrophic for mother and baby. So you're not like other dynamics in this respect, and there is no such thing as divorce. Even minor separation for the purposes of career and work can be problematic."

Mating...bonding for life... Had I accidentally mated Jordan and Kade? I swallowed.

She pressed a button on the interactive table. "Merry, could you bring a glass of water please?"

Her pink-haired assistant materialized with water. Her beaming smile dropped as she noticed me. Lilly took the glass from her and sat beside me. "Cancel my next appointment please, Merry."

Lilly pressed the glass into my hand as the door shut and waited attentively while I gulped half of it down. My hands were shaking. She took the glass from me and placed it on the table before taking my hand in hers. I'd heard omegas were tactile, could sense other's emotional states and needs, and I clung to the connection without shame.

"Tolis is the home of the viral research program," she said. "The intent here was to boost dynamic numbers, particularly alpha and omegas. What we got here was largely betas, but also gammas and deltas. I've learned much over the last two years, but still not enough about what is a very rare dynamic."

"How does, ah, the mating work?"

"There's no easy way to say this, so I'm just going to give you all the pertinent facts and then you can ask questions."

"Okay." The rabbit hole was deep, and the tumbling had yet to stop.

"Deltas work in packs, usually two or three males who establish a bond, which is more often intimate in nature, prior to meeting the gamma."

I'd already surmised that Jordan and Kade were together,

and the *pack* term also fit strangely well. They were attuned to one another in their ways and actions, seamlessly working together.

"Attraction is often described as immediate when deltas and gammas meet. There are no pheromones, so it's hard to say what this might be based on, other than physical attraction. I suspect something similar to pheromones is at play, but it's undetectable by our current technical capability."

I nodded. It had certainly been immediate for me.

"During intercourse, if all pack deltas 'hook' a gamma, then the bond is formed. This leads to a frenzy, and is very similar to a heat, during which the parties are biologically compelled to engage in repeated intercourse. The hook does sound intimidating, but gammas are physically unique and suffer no lasting harm." Her cheeks took on a little color. "I've been told it's extremely pleasurable for gammas, much like an omega enjoys an alpha's knot. It's impossible for a gamma to fall pregnant by other dynamics. I only know of two who married beta males, and in both cases, medical assistance was required."

"How do more than one hook?" I muttered before lifting a hand. "No, it's okay, I can guess." No wonder Kade had been so obsessed with taking my ass! Although he hadn't followed through. "I met two during the attack on the space station."

"You did?" Lilly said, her voice slightly high in a way that revived the tumbling sensation.

"Yes," I said slowly. No point in pretenses. Lilly knew more than me about deltas and gammas, and my instincts insisted I know everything. "We were trapped for several hours together in an agriculture pod. We were, ah, intimate." I'd managed one mind-blowing hook from Kade and one blowjob for Jordan before his insider man had messaged to say help was imminent. Jordan had definitely not hooked my throat. I shuddered. No way I'd have missed that. "We didn't bond, though." God, could this conversation be any more awkward? My face had heated to supernova level, and I couldn't see that changing soon. "Only one of them hooked me."

She had gone unnaturally still, and I didn't need to be a therapist for it to be ringing a lot of bells.

"I wasn't told of this," she said, brows pinched with concern. "The report said you had escaped the conflict behind a drop door."

"I did, eventually. I was in the canteen when the raiders arrived. They were shooting everyone in sight. I ran...straight into two men, whom I presumed to be alphas. It was only later, after we were safe behind a drop door, that I found out otherwise. They seemed to know immediately that I was a gamma, but I was clueless about their dynamic status. It was a heat of the moment thing, the danger, the death... I guess I wasn't thinking straight. I thought they might be soldiers. I know some join the war efforts, although it's not mandatory. On reflection, I believe they might have been private security for one of the mining operations. They had someone helping them who had access to the station surveillance cameras."

Her fingers tightened over mine. "I'm so sorry, I've been insensitive. I can't believe this was missing from my report."

"I didn't put it in the report," I said, feeling guilty. "I was told the information provided was voluntary."

"That's okay," she said quietly. "I'm less concerned about the report, which you are quite right, is voluntary. Although I'm sure you're self-aware enough to seek independent therapy after such an experience."

"Then what are you concerned about?" I asked, because clearly, she was, and the hole into which I'd tumbled was only getting deeper.

"Have you had contact with them since?"

"No?"

"Do you want to?"

I heaved a breath. "No," I said, although it lacked sincerity.

An uncomfortable silence followed, but I held my tongue, knowing she would speak when she was ready.

"Alphas are territorial toward omegas under their care," she said at length. "Deltas are exponentially more so when it comes to gammas, harboring a primitive and arguably unhealthy sense of ownership over compatible breeding stock. Deltas are relentless, determined, and single-minded in their quest to claim a mate, and are not above breaking laws or people who stand in their way. If even one of them hooked you, I would expect them to be back. Should you share a similar desire to further the relationship, then I have some material that will help you navigate their enthusiasm. If not, then I would suggest you file an intergalactic restraining order at the earliest opportunity."

I swallowed as I digested that deluge of information. "Do restraining orders help a great deal?" My voice sounded high and anxious, but I thought I already knew the answer.

"No," she said. "But they can provide a little breathing space."

Chapter Seven

Abby

The military base I'd been staying at was a far cry from the lovely consulting rooms where I'd met Lilly in the city. *Functional* was the best way to describe my office, from the gray walls to the strange rubbery floor and the small window that existed in a state of constant filth, such that the base compound beyond it was lost under the grime.

As I stared out that battered window at the industry of soldiers jogging out to load up onto a troop carrier, I reflected on the data pack Lilly had provided.

The only way I could be bred was during the frenzy and when hooked by my mated deltas. Yes, the article actually used the word *bred*, boldly stated in black and white. Clearly, it had been written by a man.

Only now, from the perspective of experience, I thought it might have been an accurate term for the animalistic nature of sex between deltas and gammas.

Despite reading the information Lilly provided several

times, I was still wallowing in denial. I thought about Jordan and Kade often, was curious about them and my response to them. I'd convinced myself that they were sweet, that they weren't about to embark on a quest to see me bred just because we had shared intimacy once, yet everything I read in the reports suggested otherwise. There wasn't a dipping your toes in the water option with deltas, and they didn't offer a getting to know you stage. Lilly's blunt explanation still haunted me, as did those reports backing up her words.

I'd trusted in the data and filed a restraining order, with some assistance from Lilly's team to find Jordan and Kade's full names and details of their home base.

It was time to put the episode behind me and focus on what next. Soon, I would be boarding an intergalactic vessel to Chimera. I was looking forward to seeing my parents and friends. My three-month field trip to several bases, had blown out to nearly four. But I'd been offered a position consulting to the military headquarters when I returned and was looking forward to getting back to normal.

Also, I felt it wouldn't hurt to move as far as possible from the infamous space station and the mining operation where I'd met Jordan and Kade. They were not part of the military, and few private individuals had the funds for long-distance space travel.

Once I was safely back on Chimera, I could process what had happened. I had a career and clients who relied on me being there for them. In a small way, I wanted to leave the world a better place for being in it. My life aspirations were deeply entrenched in my personality and sense of self. Giving everything up to bond for life with men I barely knew, even as powerfully erotic as the sex had been, would be nothing short of crazy.

Lilly had offered me a dossier on the two men, but I'd

declined. The less I knew, the better. In weak moments, I was tempted and curious, but I also remembered the feral pull that had sparked between us and was terrified that I might lose all common sense and beg them to breed me.

Yet despite these assumptions on their interest, another part of me, the insecure one that hid behind clothing two sizes too big, questioned whether they wanted me at all. Sure, they'd liked what was under my clothes, or had seemed to, but I was still me—a too serious woman with poor clothing style and glasses. No one wore glasses anymore.

My watch bleeped. "Ryker's here to see you, Abby," the consulting administrator announced. "Are you ready for him now?"

"Yes, please send him in." I returned to my desk and opened my data tablet, ready. Ryker, my last appointment of the day, whistled as he entered, with his dark blond hair, movie-style good looks, and one hundred percent alpha vibe.

I mentally sighed. It was going to be one of those days, I could tell. "Have a seat, Ryker," I said, drumming up a professional smile.

Unlike many of my clients, Ryker was privately funded by his father, a military general. I could only assume Pop wanted to keep Ryker's therapy off the books, which was perfectly legal. I had several clients who self-funded their therapy sessions. For confidentiality reasons, I couldn't disclose details of sessions unless the individual was subject to a criminal investigation, at which point records must be submitted. Either way, some people preferred to keep their therapy private.

In Ryker's case, his father doubtless wanted damage control over his son, a high-functioning psychopath. If the military hadn't scooped Ryker up, I was sure the results would have been worse, and they weren't great in the military.

He plopped himself down in the seat opposite, leaned

forward, and planted his forearms on his knees. "So, tell me about the deltas," he said in that soft, patient way that was all part of his façade.

I blinked a few times. How...why...who?

"No thank you."

"Abby," he said softly, now coaxing as he gestured between us. "How long have we known each other? I can't believe you're keeping secrets like this from me. I'm disappointed you didn't tell me yourself. I had to beat the shit out of Jerry to get the details, which was a very laborious process. He told me all kinds of things I really don't care about before we got to the good parts." He leaned back casually. "Is it serious? Fuck, I mean it must be serious. I'm just putting it out there, you can count on me to be discreet if you need them gotten rid of."

"Ryker, you have another infringement on your file," I said bluntly. "Can you tell me about that?"

"Nope." He shook his head. "Don't think I can. I mean, it wasn't technically an infringement, more of a misunderstanding."

"It's here in black and white," I said, holding up a piece of actual paper with chicken scrawl handwriting on it. Who even used paper anymore? I frowned at the writing, belatedly reading the word 'Jerry.' I blanched. "Please tell me this isn't to do with me."

He grinned and winked. "Absolutely nothing to do with you."

I picked up my data tablet and began to tap away.

His smirk dropped. "You'll still be my therapist on Chimera, right?"

Chapter Eight

Jordan

"**I** can't believe she filed a restraining order," Kade said as he strapped up his hands, ready for our sparring session. We had the gym to ourselves. The only other people who used it were Lucian and his asshole hacker, the Gecko. We'd just gotten off an uneventful shift in the club, and Lucian had turned in. The Gecko had never once shown himself, so I wasn't expecting him either, although it would make my fucking day if he did.

I owed the bastard for sending us on a merry chase all over the universe. I owed him for a lot of things, but I'd cut him a bit of slack because we'd met Abby as a result, and he'd gotten us somewhere safe when raiders were shooting shit up.

"I can," I replied, not that I was going to let a restraining order stop me. Fuck no. We worked for a ruthless criminal. We'd gotten our hands dirty plenty and had no issues crossing lines again. Little gamma was already ours. We were just playing a game until the inevitable caught up.

Kade grinned as he began shadow boxing to warm up. "She's classy and smart, I could tell straight away, and damn if she wasn't wet dreams level of hot under that dress. Probably has snooty financial advisors begging for a taste of her pussy. No way is she giving herself over to us. We're going to have to work for the prize."

I grunted as I pulled the binding tape out of my bag and began to wind it over my knuckles.

The gym was deep in the basement beneath Peppermint Moon, a fancy club owned by the equally fancy and indisputably corrupt Lucien Banner, aka our boss. The windowless room was decked out with state-of-the-art equipment, boasted icy air conditioning, and a good amount of floor space for sparring and such. Our apartment was situated several floors above Peppermint Moon and came with the job, along with furnishings, enough black pants and shirts to last a lifetime, and top-notch medical care. Then there were the weapons. Lucian did not skimp on quality weapons, while the medical cover was a sensible inclusion, given the physical nature of our work.

It suited us, both of us, because we were deltas and we did everything together...including pursuing sweet gammas.

"I need sugar," I muttered, stalking over to the big cooler and pushing aside the fancy water Lucian preferred for a juice. I was feeling edgy. I was always feeling edgy, so this was nothing new.

"What are we going to do about it?" Kade demanded, pausing his shadow boxing to stretch out.

I put the juice down. I enjoyed the sugar hit but it wasn't a great idea to guzzle it down right before exercise. Kade had already worked up a little sweat, and it glistened on his bare chest. He'd been pushing himself extra hard since we returned, burning off tension in the gym, and he was seriously ripped.

He was watching me, ever a predator, but he also deferred

to me, despite being a big bastard and arguably my physical superior.

I went through a few kickboxing moves myself, feeling the blood begin to pump and my awareness sharpen as I mulled over the answer to his question of what we would do about Abby and her fucking restraining order. Brat was going to get her ass spanked for that little stunt at some point, but that was for later—after she was safe under our care.

I took up a position opposite Kade, fists loose and up, arms braced, ready. "Whatever it takes," I replied. Right fist curving, I went for the first tap.

He blocked it easily, danced back, and came in with a jab. I dipped to the side, and it landed on my shoulder, knocking me back a step. We were only warming up. Bastard needed to ease up on the fucking weights.

"You think she's the one?" he asked, coming in with a series of light moves that I blocked or dodged.

I growled low and deep back in the throat, went in with a left-right jab, and followed it up with a hook kick. "Do you have any doubts?"

He shook his head. "No, not me. You just, you know, don't give much away, and I needed to know you're all in."

I relaxed my shoulders a fraction. "I'm fucking in, asshole. Now, let's step this shit up. Got some rage to work through."

He grinned and came at me thick and fast. I dodged and blocked a few, but plenty got through, and we were soon both breathing hard.

The dull pain soothed me, a blanket slowly enfolding me and taking the noise from my mind. It was exactly what I needed, and I lost myself in the rhythm unique to combat. I couldn't get *her* out of my mind, though, and the pain only narrowed my focus. The dynamic differences between alphas-omegas and deltas-gammas were worlds apart, for all we looked so similar. There was no pheromone hit nor heat, although a psychic connection could be formed, I'd heard. It wasn't like I'd spoken to many other deltas. The information had been given to me by a doctor at the orphanage where we'd stayed, and to be blunt, he'd known fuck all. I'd picked up some more stuff on the underweb over the years, but I doubted it provided the whole picture.

They had programs in place for alphas and omegas, training that gave them everything they needed for their path through life. The omegas trained in submission and alphas in control. No one bothered to do that for deltas, except maybe in the military, but neither Kade nor I had been interested in that path. We could be aggressive, but we weren't unhinged in the way that alphas were, in general. Well, we weren't supposed to be, but I guessed I was the exception.

We'd both put our shitty childhoods behind us as best as we could. Understanding why you turned out the way you did, didn't always help you to change it, but I'd learned to temper the less congenial aspects to my personality...*mostly.*

"Tiring yet, old man?" Kade taunted.

Asshole! I needed a lot more pain before I calmed the beast inside, the one that couldn't stand that *she* was somewhere else, independent, away from us and our protection, where any bastard might be sniffing around. The ants were under my skin again. I needed her under me, with my hook buried deep, that hot pussy milking me. I needed the pain to clear my head, and after, I might be able to find a plan, because without one, I'd likely do something crazy like get on a spaceship bound for Tolis, which would piss our boss off and likely land our asses in prison.

Our other boss would be even less impressed.

The next punch nearly took my head off, and I landed on my ass.

I waved a hand in submission and heaved breath. I was hot, sweaty, and sore all over, but I wasn't close to clearing the buzz.

Kade stalked over to the cooler to grab water as I heaved myself to my feet. He eyeballed me over the bottle with a brooding expression, like he knew all the dark shit that was careening through my mind. He grimaced and shook his head. "Got that eye twitch going on there, buddy. Wanna talk about it?"

I didn't do fucking emotions, so asking me if I wanted to talk about something was a sure way to wind me up. "No, I'm not fucking okay. I've not been okay a day in my life. I fucking need her where I can see her."

His lips tugged up. He was big, handsome, and fucking cocky. I loved him. Kade had my back. I might have saved his scrawny ass back at the orphanage, but he'd saved mine too, every fucking day. If it weren't for Kade, I'd probably be locked up somewhere or dead.

"You mean where you can fuck her?" he taunted, smirking.

I closed the distance between us, and his nostrils flared as I took him by the throat. He was a couple of inches taller than me and had at least twenty pounds of extra muscle, but I was the most dominant and he'd never once challenged me.

His face flushed from the exertion and from what I was doing. I squeezed just hard enough to make a point, feeling the heat coming off his body as I pushed right into him until we almost touched.

My eyes lowered to where his cock pointed straight up, rigid behind his exercise pants.

"Is that for the hot little gamma or me?"

"Both," he said honestly. "It's definitely both."

I shoved the band of his sweats down, exposing his cock.

He hissed. "Jesus Christ, Jordan. The fucking asshole Gecko is probably fucking watching."

"Shut the fuck up." I pinned him with a look as I wrapped my fist around him. "Don't come."

His chest heaved as I jacked my fist up and down, swiping my thumb over the leaking pre-cum, reveling in the power. He began trembling, needing to get off hard and fast, but I was feeling cruel, and he was gonna have to wait.

He grunted when I released him, but it turned into a groan when I brought my thumb to my mouth and sucked the taste of him off. He didn't move, just stood there, chest heaving, cock out, waiting for instruction.

It was always like this between us. He was the other half of me, and for so long, I'd never needed anything else, had been sure I didn't need a woman permanently, gamma or otherwise, although we'd shared a few.

Until Abby slammed into us.

Now, I was fucking obsessed.

"Whatever it takes," I said, meeting his gaze head-on as I closed my hand around his shaft again. "We know how to work the system. We'll find her, and when we do, little gamma won't stand a chance. She'll be ours to enjoy, whenever and wherever we want. I want to wake up every morning and watch her worship my cock, feel her trembling against me as you take her from behind."

"Fuck, Jordan," he rumbled. "I'm fucking close."

"On your knees."

He fell to his knees, didn't hesitate to yank my pants down, and closed his mouth around my length, sucking me straight to the back of his throat.

I threw a look toward the ceiling and groaned. Fuck, he was good at this, but I supposed he'd had enough practice. The sensation of his hot, wet mouth around me and the swirl of his tongue sent me spinning. I imagined Abby watching him do this. Would she be shocked? Would she like it?

"Hands off your cock," I snarled.

He did as he was told. He'd learned long ago that not following my instructions led to my full abstinence from proceedings. He was a needy bastard and hated when I didn't play.

"I'm going to come, and you're going to swallow it down like the greedy cum junkie you are."

Kade didn't miss a beat, sucking me deeper and doing that magic twirling thing with his tongue that had me seeing stars. My mind digressed to the image of Abby kneeling sweetly beside him, waiting for her turn...and I came.

"Fuck!" I muttered gruffly. I felt like the top of my head was coming off as I shot load after load down his throat. He sucked it down, a low rumble in his chest of pleasure. Kade was a giver, and he got off on pleasing me. By the time my balls were drained, my legs were weak as cooked noodles but my head was clear at last.

"Up," I rumbled. "Definitely need somewhere private for what I have in mind."

We threw our T-shirts on and made out like a couple of horny teenagers in the elevator back to our apartment. Once behind closed doors, we stripped and got in the shower together, where I lubed up his ass and fucked him under the pelting hot water against the stall wall.

Physically and emotionally drained after, we went to bed, and as per normal, I lay on my back while Kade threw his heavy arm over my waist and fell straight asleep.

I didn't. I just lay there going over all the facts. First things first, we needed to find out where she was. Lucian would have to build a fucking bridge, because this took priority.

I was starting to doze when my watch buzzed with an incoming message.

Kade grunted and rolled over, but I smiled. He did not like

shit messing with his sleep, which was too bad for him because in our line of work, it happened frequently.

I squinted at my watch. *The Gecko?* The fuck did he want?

Rolling out of the bed, I padded over to the big window that looked out across the city of Chimera. It was early morning, but dull and gray. The skyscrapers, stretching out as far as the eye could see, were alive with flashing, twinkling lights.

This had better be fucking good.

I hit the comms. "Sup?"

"So," he began. *"It came to my attention that a certain gamma by the name of Abby Winters just landed on Chimera. Thought you might like to know. Therapist, class one, got a job at military headquarters here. Deals with the tricky fuckers—aka the psychos. So just saying, you're up against some stiff competition. Might want to move fast before another dark and twisted catches her eye."* I growled into the communicator. *"Jez! Lighten up, asshole! By the way, now you owe me. You're welcome."*

The fucker hung up.

I glared at my watch.

Then I chuckled.

Then I went back to bed and slept like a baby.

I woke up to Kade sucking on my cock. Forcing bleary eyes open, I found him propped on one elbow, one hand holding my meat to his lips, the other jacking up and down his big dick.

"I'm going to come," I rumbled, feeling the heat sweep through my body, the tingling sensation at the base of my spine that said release was inevitable.

The bastard pulled his lips off with an exaggerated pop, and I growled at him. He grinned and crawled onto his knees between my thighs, then thrust his cock against mine. "I want to come together," he said, eyes locked on where our cocks rubbed together.

I closed my fist around the two of us, squeezed just a little too roughly, and worked up and down.

"Fuck! Jesus!" he muttered, although he didn't tell me to stop.

"She's here," I said, feeling my balls tighten. Kade had done quite a number warming me up.

"What?" he asked, still riveted by the image of our mashed cocks, ruddy and leaking a sticky trail of pre-cum all over my abs.

"Abby Winters arrived in Chimera last night, and I know where she works."

"Ah, fuck!"

He came, and I followed him straight over, mouth open on a low groan as I jacked ropey cum all over my belly and chest.

"Fuck! Fucking yes. Fuck! I'm going to come again."

He didn't. Instead, he all but bounded off the bed and hit the shower, leaving me a sticky mess on the bed.

I grinned.

For reasons that suited both our bosses, our registered home planet was Ridious. No way Abby would have come here if she'd realized where we lived. Our gamma was about to get one hell of a surprise.

Chapter Nine

Abby

"We were going to wait until your next birthday," my mother said as we shared breakfast in the conservatory of their five-story townhouse. "But your father thought it was time."

I looked between them, wondering what was coming. They weren't terrible parents, but they were thetas and didn't really do empathy or emotions, while I did them all. We were dynamic polar opposites.

Before us, a stone topped table, large enough to seat twelve with ease, was laden with sweet and savory morning food of every conceivable variety, complete with an extravagant floral centerpiece.

I put my half eaten pastry on my plate, dabbed the crumbs from my lips with the linen napkin, and mentally braced myself.

"We put aside some money," my father said. "We always

hoped you would follow us into business, but we have come to accept your needs are different. We happened to mention to a friend of ours that you were returning to Chimera and had been offered a position consulting to the military headquarters here. He'd recently passed up on an apartment within a good commuting distance, so we took the liberty of purchasing it and believe it might fit your requirements. Our property manager negotiated an excellent price, so if you don't like it, we can always sell it on."

My mouth was hanging open, and I must have looked as attractive as a dead fish. I snapped my mouth shut and pushed my glasses up my nose. I felt tears sting the back of my eyes. They had just bought an apartment for me. It struck me that in their quiet way, they were proud of me, that they had been talking to an acquaintance about me suggested as much. I was staying in my old room here, but it was impractical to commute to my new job, and I'd planned to start researching rentals today.

"You bought me an apartment?" I said slowly.

"Yes, darling," my mother said, bestowing me with a rare smile. "After everything that happened, we're just happy to have you home and want you to be comfortable and feel safe. The complex use Brownwells for their security, which is arguably the best you can get on Chimera."

"Wow," I offered inadequately. I'd heard somewhere that Brownwells handled the security for the big casinos and clubs. I didn't realize they also managed apartment buildings. Then again, it wasn't like I'd ever looked at the fancier residences, of which this apartment was clearly one. I was delighted and a little wary that they had taken the process and choice from me. "Where is it?"

"Westgate," my mother stated proudly. "It overlooks the

river and is close to the local transport hub to make commuting easy."

My eyes widened. "That is amazing." I'd been dreading searching for a new home, truth be told. Westgate was a prestigious suburb I'd dismissed from my rental research even before I arrived. "Thank you so much."

My mother reached across the table and squeezed my hand gently. They weren't affectionate, but they understood that I was and had always tried. It must have been so hard for them to have a child so different from them in every way, one that presented new challenges at every age and stage of my development.

People could say what they liked about thetas, that they were cold, ruthless, and concerned only about money, and they were to some extent. But they were also hyper-intelligent, and they'd always done their best for me.

"I can't wait to see it."

"Damien said he would take you over after breakfast," my father said as I reached for my pastry.

I was already committed to taking a bite of the excellent pastry, but it turned to dust in my mouth. My brother, Damien, was a theta like my parents, but while my parents were the milder version of the caste, my brother personified the darkest, most ruthless traits prevalent in their kind. It wasn't so much that we didn't get along, more that our circles of interest were so wildly different, no point of commonality could be found.

"He did?" I asked after swallowing the lump of food with an effort.

"Yes," my mother said. "I was surprised, but he's been trying lately, putting a great deal of time and effort into socializing outside his caste. I think you'll find he's changed while you've been away."

I'd been gone exactly five months and I couldn't believe

he'd changed that much, but I nodded and picked up my coffee. Damien and I hadn't spoken once since I'd left. Even after the space station attack, he hadn't so much as sent a polite inquiry on my well-being. Despite my mother professing that he had changed, I was immediately suspicious that there was more than brotherly love involved in his desire to show me around my new apartment.

Was he bitter that they'd given me this gift? No, I don't think he was, but something was going on. Older than me by two years, he had already accumulated considerable wealth. Unlike my parents, whose interests were primarily in financial securities, my brother, unusually for a theta, had branched into intergalactic trading. He spent much of his time away. I was surprised to find Damien on Chimera at all.

The conservatory door opened as I was mulling over this development, and my brother entered the room. He had an average height, slim build, dark hair from my father, and green eyes from my mother. Like me, he wore glasses due to a genetic defect, one that couldn't be corrected without risks we'd been disinclined toward taking.

"Abigail," he said. "What a pleasure to see you."

His smile lacked any nuance of emotion as he leaned in to kiss my cheek, but I appreciated that he tried. "Likewise, Damien. How have you been?"

"Good," he said. "I've been good. I heard you had quite an adventure while you were in space. Glad to have you back safe."

So he had acknowledged it, at least. "Thank you."

"Will you have some breakfast?" my mother asked.

"No, thank you," he declined politely. "If Abigail's ready, I'll take her to the apartment."

"She's barely started," my mother said, indicating the spread.

"No, really, I'm full," I said, confident I wouldn't get anything past my lips while Damien watched. "I'm excited to see the apartment." Whatever his agenda in making this offer, I wanted to get it over with.

"Have fun," my father said. Yeah, that wasn't going to happen. "Let us know how you get on."

"I will," I said. "I'm sure I'm going to love it."

We left, heading out the back of the house for the skycar parking garage.

"Is that supposed to be a dress?" Damien asked, side-eyeing me. "I see your taste in clothing hasn't improved much during your travels."

I laughed. "I see your manners haven't improved much either, despite Mother telling me you were a changed man."

"Touché," he said, lips tugging up in a smirk. "You'll like the apartment. They have excellent taste. It's huge, fully furnished, and comes with its own butler."

"I-I don't want a butler," I spluttered as I slid into the skycar beside him. It was a sleek modern affair. I had no doubt that it cost more than my apartment.

He winked. "Just joking about the butler, although it's so big, you might wish you had one." He took the controls, and we rose smoothly into the air, then shot off at a speed that had me clinging to the seat.

He chuckled. "You never did like excitement, did you?"

"No," I said, clutching the armrest for dear life. "Please slow down. I have no desire to die today."

"This model has an impeccable safety record," he said. "It's pretty much indestructible."

"I don't want to test that theory, thank you, Damien."

He smirked and slowed to a regular speed.

I unpeeled my fingers from the armrest.

"I heard you're working with alphas," he said as he directed the skycar into a transport stream and switched to autopilot.

"I do," I say. "Sometimes, among other dynamics."

"Don't know how you can stand to be around them. They're aggressive and full of their own importance." He rubbed his jaw and propped an elbow on the armrest. "Doesn't it bother you, working with them? Or do you delude yourself that you can fix them?"

"Not all alphas need therapy," I said, "and no, it doesn't bother me working with them. If it did, I would do something else."

He shrugged. "The Empire would be a better place without them. Thank god you didn't turn out to be an omega."

I frowned. "What's wrong with omegas?"

"They're slaves to alphas for a start."

I shook my head. "No, I don't think that they are. I believe changes are coming. Omegas are gaining independence."

"Change?" His look was skeptical. "Give me one example of an omega that isn't bound to an alpha? We're all slaves to the alphas. You know that don't you? Merely minions to be used, even thetas, who are arguably their intellectual superiors."

"Lillian Brach," I said.

"The governor's daughter?" he asked, frowning.

"Yes. I met her on Tolis. She works in the viral research program." I felt a lot like I was grasping at straws. Lilly was the only omega I knew who wasn't with an alpha, which wasn't a compelling body of evidence.

"Her father is an alpha on the ruling council, so she hardly counts. Not that she's independent anymore. Didn't you hear the news?"

I shook my head, a cold skittering sensation trickling down my spine.

"The capital of Tolis was destroyed in an Uncorrupted

attack. The doctor was taken, or so my inside man told me. It's all being kept hush-hush."

"What?" My heart was in my throat, and my earlier pastry and coffee felt like lead in my stomach. I'd been there and might have been taken, while Lillian had. The thought of the kind doctor in the Uncorrupted's hands made me shudder in horror.

"Oh, she's safe now," he continued, smirking. "Daddy's position on the ruling council saw to that. They sent the big guns in, and black ops specialists plucked her right off an Uncorrupted ship. Everyone else was left to the tender mercy of the Uncorrupted, but the doctor is safe and sound, so that's all that matters to the ruling council."

The bitterness that laced his tone might have been justified in this case. My parents were thetas, and while unquestionably wealthy, they did not hold sway over the military, nor did I presume special consideration might have been taken for me.

"She's safe now?" I felt terrible asking for her well-being when so many others were prisoners and suffering.

He shrugged. "In a way. They've allocated her two controllers, so it's fair to presume Daddy's not taking any chances with her safety. I believe one of them is on your books —a Ryker Sherwin."

"Oh god," I muttered weakly, because despite briefly considering how wonderful they might look together, I couldn't think of a worse match for an omega who'd just gone through a traumatic experience. Also, how did Damien even know who was or wasn't on my books?

"No, not a god," he said dryly. "He's an alpha, and like all of that caste, he probably thinks he's superior to god. Do you think you might get to meet him?"

"Who?" I was still grappling with the idea of Lilly being

assigned to Ryker and another unknown controller. How would that even work?

"Ryker," he elaborated. "They're on route to Chimera. The whole viral research program is being relocated here."

"You can't seriously expect me to talk about my clients. How do you even know who's on my books? And how do you know about an attack that hasn't been on the news?"

He shrugged. "I had offices on Tolis, so I know first-hand about the attack. As for Ryker, a lucky guess. I presumed every alpha needed therapy...or a lobotomy. I might seem aloof, but I've followed your career very closely. You have an excellent reputation, and gammas are much coveted as therapists, even so. Godfrey Sherwin is a general, probably best friends with Governor Brach given his son's now Lillian Brach's controller. Stands to reason a man with that level of influence would want the best therapist for his psycho son."

His compliment was a jarring note against the other revelations. I'd had no idea he even knew what I did, never mind the nuances of my career.

"Not that one can do much for an alpha of any variety. At least the soldiers are honest and useful. If they stayed as military grunts, the Empire would be an infinitely better place. Those food riots down at the docks, did you hear about that? Poor management by the government, and not just Chimera, it's the same on every world. They don't have the appetite for the difficult decisions that need to be made. No, better if alphas didn't aspire to be more than trained killers. Leave the politics to their betters."

"And who are their betters? Thetas? Are you thinking about going into politics?" I asked. "I thought you were focused on building your company."

"Politics? No, there's no place for thetas in politics beyond the middle tiers. I think it's time there was a change, though.

What do you think about that, Abby? A new ruling elite based on capability."

I thought about my parents, measured thetas, who could see beyond their own caste for my sake. I thought many thetas were capable of governance, but I also thought too many of any single caste inevitably led to corruption. Alphas had always formed the upper tier of governance. I shrugged. "Dynamic diversity makes sense, and at every level."

"Diversity?" he scoffed. "Thetas are the most intelligent. It should go to those most capable."

"Are you?" I asked.

His face darkened. "Absolutely we're the most intelligent. It's well documented. Even the lowest thetas leave other dynamics for dust."

"There are many levels of intelligence," I said. "And many scales on which people can be measured. Emotional intelligence for one. Thetas naturally lack such skills."

"Emotional intelligence just gets in the way," he said, switching the skycar to manual and exiting the transport stream.

His words settled heavily between us. He was right—the ruling elite shouldn't be wholly alphas, but I also thought it shouldn't be wholly thetas. Unless he was merely playing devil's advocate, proposing another extreme to emphasize the current inequality. Only with Damien, I couldn't be sure.

I was distracted from my musings when Westgate came into view, a beautiful riverfront suburb full of glistening towers soaring high. Of course we landed on the rooftop parking garage of the tallest building.

"Only the best for the darling daughter," Damien said, grinning.

The strange coldness I'd felt while discussing matters in the skycar eased, and my former brother returned. "You have the energy to make changes if you wished," I said as he powered the skycar down. "You could be the first theta of the ruling elite. You could help them to see dynamic diversity benefits us all. Think about what someone like a mu could bring, the perspective that they might have."

"Mu?" he scoffed as we headed through the double doors, finding a plush setting and a bank of elevators.

He swiped the call, and the doors sprung open with a happy bong.

"Mus have no stomach for what needs to be done," he said. "No, I simply cannot imagine a mu on the ruling council. It would be an absolute disaster."

"But betas could bring a different perspective," I thought aloud.

"Oh, please," he said as the elevator ascended slowly. "Next you'll be suggesting non-dynamics. You know there's a reason they're non-dynamics."

"If everybody were a theta, it would be a very boring world," I pointed out.

The elevator stopped, and the doors slid open, revealing a passage with subtle lighting and plush carpets underfoot.

"It would be incredibly boring," he agreed. "But a world where the thetas ruled, that would be magnificent indeed."

The apartment was every bit as palatial as Damien had suggested. He showed me around, explaining the security system and various other features and fixtures, then a call came for him and he needed to leave. He asked if I wanted to be returned to our parents' house or if I wished to stay here.

I opted to stay. It was close to the transport hub, as my

parents had mentioned, and I could easily return later for my things.

Alone, I wandered through the tastefully presented rooms, thoughts turning over what Damien had just said.

There had been a time, not very long ago, on that fateful space station, when I looked my own death in the eye. If not for two deltas, I believed I would be dead, my parents mourning me and this beautiful apartment home to somebody else.

The career opportunity awaiting me would have been fulfilling someone else's dream.

My parents were unquestionably wealthy, so maybe money had not motivated me because of that. What interested me was people. I found great satisfaction in providing a framework of care that allowed people to understand their emotions, to accept themselves and their limitations and scars, to move past them, and be a better, happier version of themselves.

As I flopped back on the decadent couch that could have seated ten people with ease and looked out on the skyline, my thoughts turned to the two delta men I'd met on that fateful station.

I'd thought about them often in the days since we parted ways. We spent so brief a time in each other's company, yet they'd left a forever impression. Deltas were the second rarest dynamic only to mine.

We were from different worlds, literally, and it saddened me that I would never see them again, even though I knew nothing about them, save for the way they'd made me feel.

I shivered. Oh how they had made me feel so much more than I'd believed I was capable of.

I had a wonderful new home and a job I was looking forward to.

I should've felt happy.

And I did.

But circumstances had changed me. I wasn't the same gamma inspired by the simple desire to become a therapist and help people.

Raiders and two deltas had stormed into my life.

It would take me years to get over the terror of the attack and a lifetime to get over the two men who had saved me and then shown me the heights of pleasure.

Chapter Ten

Jordan

"You want a therapist?" Lucian asked in the manner of a man confused, swiveling his seat so that he faced both of us. He looked like the epitome of sophistication, with immaculately styled dark hair, a sharp suit with a faint stripe, and a waistcoat underneath, making him seem like a wealthy businessman.

Technically, he was a businessman, but Lucian Banner was also a criminal with his fingers in many pies, most of which would land his and our asses in a government correction facility for more years than we had life.

We'd met many years ago, and not long after, he'd gotten out of the military. A shady bastard had crossed both of us, and we'd collaborated to take him down.

Impressed with our work, he'd offered us a job afterward. We'd already had one unofficial job, but as it turned out, they meshed nicely. We worked for Lucian with the understanding that we might be called upon to perform duties outside his control from time to time.

"I had to kill someone last week," I said seriously. "It's really been troubling me."

"Me too," Kade chipped in.

Lucian's eyebrows crawled up into his hairline as he leaned back into his chair. He had several offices. Today, we were over in his fight club, Mantis, and his windowless office had a grungy vibe with polished stone floors, exposed girders, and artfully placed spotlights accenting his desk and the low seating arrangement to his left. "What the fuck? You kill someone like every fucking week," he said, waving his cigar in our general direction before stabbing it out viciously in the ashtray on his glossy, palatial desk. He blew out a breath, and the sweet scent of cigar perfumed the air.

"Exactly," Kade said reasonably. "Who knows when we might flip if we don't get some help. They offer it in the military."

"Are you fucking with me?" Lucien's expression remained skeptical. "In case it escaped your notice, this isn't the fucking military. Did my b—Did the Gecko put you up to this?"

"Nope," Kade said. "Not at all. We just think it's sensible, ya know?"

"Because we might have to kill some fucker again," I added. "I'm comfortable feeling edgy, but it's been veering toward volatile." I wasn't lying about that—Abby and all things pertaining to claiming her had me ready to climb walls.

"Fine," Lucian said, raising both hands in surrender. "Get a fucking therapist."

"We want you to pay for it," I said. "So that it looks official."

"The fuck," Lucian muttered. "Do I look like a fucking charity? Do you not have enough clothes and toys?" He gestured in our general direction. "I'm almost afraid to ask why we need a rocket-propelled grenade launcher in inventory. Are you planning on taking out a country? Now you want fucking therapy? On my books?"

"Yep," Kade said, nodding. "All of that. Official, with your company name on it, but not our real ones—the fake names you had done for us last year."

"Jesus. Fine! I'll have my assistant find your fucking therapist. "

"We've already got one," I said, tapping my watch and then swiping my finger across to send the data to his screen.

"Abby Winters," Lucian said slowly, turning from the information to us. "Would Abby happen to be hot?"

"Off the fucking charts ho—Uff!"

I punched Kade's shoulder.

"Tell me this isn't you pursuing a woman who's not interested," Lucien said, "because I've got a lot of shit going on, and I don't need your psycho asses going off the rails."

"We want a fucking therapist," I said. "We want this one. It's not negotiable."

"Fuck me." His eyes suddenly narrowed on the screen again. "Do you know how much she costs?"

"Exactly," I said. "That's why you're paying for it and not us."

He sent us a withering glare. "Fine then. I need the pair of you over at the docks. My inside man said the players are going to be there. I want your eyes on the ground."

"On it," I said, all business now.

Chimera central cargo docks were a sprawling complex of buildings, roads, hubs, and spokes. Intergalactic shipping came through here in a constant stream as supplies were moving to and from the distant corners of the galaxy.

Our destination today was not the big, automated commercial docks nor the military docks, which were closed to the public, but the smaller docks that the independent businesses used. Like any such location, it had good and bad parts, but some sectors were rife with crime and corruption, particularly Southbank.

Barely organized chaos greeted us, with bots, movers, and human workers crisscrossing the dusty, grungy mismatch of seedy-looking company offices, dive bars, workshops, and storage units.

Work here was still manual, and alphas who avoided conscription in the military often found themselves taking such positions. Dressed as dockworkers with plain pants and shirts in a dull, buff color, we fitted right in with the diverse dynamics present.

The government, via the viral research program, had developed a drug that could turn non-dynamics into dynamics. While any dynamic was preferable over a non-dynamic, the money was in omegas and where Lucian Banner's interest lay.

Lucian already had a batch of the drug, but word was out more was shipping through. Gaining a monopoly on such an asset would be incredibly lucrative. He had labs under the guise of shampoo manufacturing that made party pills of various kinds. The omega drug, as it was dubbed, was a whole other ballgame. He was already wealthier than god, but like any businessman, corrupt or otherwise, he was always looking for the next big venture and avenue to further wealth.

It suited our other boss to keep tabs on what was going down. The government, for obvious reasons, wasn't too happy that some of their precious research had found its way out of official labs. A drug this powerful on the black market and in the hands of a man like Lucian was far from ideal, but better than the Empire's enemy, the Uncorrupted, who wanted to turn the clock back to the good old days before the virus, when humans were merely human. Their mission was to eradicate every dynamic and liberate the non-dynamics who lived in our worlds.

Lucian would monetize the drug.

The Uncorrupted would weaponize it.

It was fair to say the stakes in this shipment we were tracking were sky-high.

"I fucking love this place," Kade said as we navigated our way between raucous dock workers and ground transports throwing up dust.

I scowled at Kade. "What the fuck is wrong with you?" A fight broke out on our right, and a couple of men stumbled out of a dive bar, arms cartwheeling as they traded blows.

We were orphans, kids from the streets, who'd somehow survived. I felt comfortable here, even if it made my fucking skin crawl.

"It's just, ya know, there's a vibe about Southbank," Kade said, a mile wide grin on his face.

I cut him a scowl. "Here's the place," I said, eyeballing the dump before us. Reaper's Revenge was a particularly seedy backstreet establishment that served beer and drugs, both the legal and the illegal kind. Lucian's hacker buddy had told us a beta by the name of Mikael Sanders drank here every Thursday. Officially, he worked for a shipping company. Unofficially, he took backhands from the Uncorrupted for information and occasionally, goods.

We pushed in the dusty wooden door—real wood, like from a tree. It even creaked. "This place is fucking humming," Kade said.

I'd seen some dumps in my life, both before and after I

entered Lucian's employment, but this was a particularly ripe variety of bullshit. No one needed to bother buying drugs here when breathing the air was enough to get you stoned. Nothing fitted or matched—a bit of plastic sheeting screwed together to make the top of the bar, loose cables dangled here and there, and neon lights flashed in a way I thought had more to do with erratic power supply than for effect. Every single table and chair were different. Maybe I'd gotten used to comfort in Lucian's world, with its state-of-the-art electronics, comfortable chairs, and extra soft bedding.

Dockworkers and company personnel shouted at one another over the electronic music.

Fuck, I felt old.

"If you're fucking playing us again," I snarled into my communicator. "I'm going to find you and rip out your throat."

"The space station wasn't my fault," the Gecko said. *"I already explained that. Technically, you being there was my fault. In my defense, how was I to know raiders would turn up and start shooting shit up?"*

"Ah, buddy, you got that eye twitching thing happening," Kade said, patting me on the shoulder. "I'll get us a drink."

We worked our way over to the bar.

A scruffy-looking bartender, complete with a black leather patch over one eye, nodded his head at us. "What can I get ya?" he asked, wiping his hand down his stained T-shirt.

"Beer," Kade said.

"Orange juice," I said.

The bartender raised his brow.

"What the fuck is your problem?" I muttered.

"Don't get many juice orders here," he said, grabbing a beer for Kade out of the cooler. "That a fancy new drug? I've not heard that."

"It's a fucking juice," I said through gritted teeth. "It tastes like orange."

He nodded before shuffling off to rummage in a cabinet at the back end of the bar, returning shortly later with a juice. He made a show of wiping the dust off the bottle with his T-shirt, snapped the lid off, and slammed it on the bar in front of me.

"Do you not have a fucking glass?"

Kade nudged me and leaned in. "Let's wind it back a notch, buddy, and get the table over on the back wall."

I grunted my agreement, and we found a table out of the way, where we could observe.

Mikael Sanders finally turned up three incredibly dull hours and four orange juices later. A small beta with sandy blond hair, grubby clothes, and a twitchy disposition, he fitted in perfectly.

He nodded at the bartender and passed something over. Cash maybe? Hard to see from here. The bartender handed him a beer and a small package, which Sanders slipped into his pocket.

"What was that about?" Kade asked.

"Could be fucking anything," I replied. "Might be nothing more than his favorite drug." I tapped my communicator. "Are you still there, asshole?"

"*Of course I'm fucking here,*" the Gecko replied. "*Bored fucking witless. Anything exciting happened yet?*"

"Sanders is here. He took a small package from the bartender before heading toward the back, where he's talking to a couple of his buddies. They weren't particularly discreet about it. Could be no one gives a fuck here, or it was nothing important. Want us to shake him down?"

"*No,*" the Gecko said. "*Not today. According to reports, the drug's not on Chimera yet. If we move too soon, we're busted and we've lost the opportunity. Just observe. See if you can tag who he's talking to. If you can tag Sanders, even better."*

"Will do," I replied.

A fight broke out near the bar, a couple of lugs slugging it out over a spilled drink. Everybody whooped it up. When they'd finished brawling like a couple of drunk sloths, the bartender nodded his head at the twitchy security guard who'd done fuck all so far, and he hefted the unconscious bastard out.

The tracker devices Lucian's hacker supplied were tiny pieces of cybernetic equipment that could integrate with the fabric—time for us to use it.

"I'm on Sanders," Kade said. "You hang out by the bar and see if the others come past."

As Sanders walked by, Kade headed for the bar, bumping into the smaller man.

"Sorry," he said, holding both hands up, copping a look from Sanders.

Given Kade towered over Sanders, that was as far as it went. He didn't look at me, just stalked for the door. I guessed he'd done the job he wanted to.

I wasted a few minutes, trying to gain the bartender's attention so we could pay off our tab.

When I turned back, the others had slipped out the back—opportunity missed.

I nodded my head in that direction. "What's out there?" I asked the bartender.

"None of your fucking business."

I raised a brow. "Fair enough. You might have noticed I don't drink, but I like something a little more of a buzz."

"Not today," the bartender said. "Sold the last. You come back next week. I'll have some then."

I nodded and left.

"Did you do it?" Kade asked. He was leaning against the wall outside and fell into step beside me.

"No, they slipped out the back," I said.

"What's out the back?" he asked.

"Don't know. I asked the bartender. He said it was none of my fucking business."

"You better get the Gecko on that," Kade said. "I got the tracker on Sanders. Let's see if it yields anything."

Chapter Eleven

Abby

I'd settled into my life, apartment, and new job with surprising ease, almost like I'd never left Chimera. I caught up with my friends, and resumed my therapy work.

I was delighted all round.

I wasn't delighted about the practice manager informing me that a refurbishment was about to commence, and our current consulting suite would be unavailable for several weeks while the work was done.

"This has been planned for months," Cora said, a capable beta with a no-nonsense attitude.

"Where are we moving to?" I asked. I was already on first name terms with the barista in the beautiful coffee shop several floors below. The handsome beta male always greeted me with a smile and usually slipped a free mini cookie in with the order.

"It's a lower floor of this building, a former suite of medical consulting rooms," Cora said before adding with a grimace,

"I'm afraid as a junior member of our practice, you've drawn the short straw."

"Of course," I said. I had the smallest room now, and it didn't bother me. If anything, I found it cozy. "When are we moving into them?"

"First thing Monday morning. The rooms are already prepared for us. Do feel free to pop over and have a look when it's convenient. I'll send you the details."

I put the matter aside, and I didn't pop over. Like Cora said, I was a junior practice member, and I'd make do with whatever I got.

Then Monday morning came around, and I understood the full magnitude of drawing the short straw.

The first thing I noticed was the bright, borderline neon, color scheme in the small waiting room.

"Wow," I said, turning full circle, wondering at the designer's skill in making every single thing clash. I was prepared for worse when I pushed open my office door. The lime green walls and cherry red matching couches perfectly met my abysmal expectations.

I wasn't sure how my clients would feel having therapy in the room. I'd been here mere minutes, and it was giving me a headache.

A chuckle bubbled up with the edge of hysteria.

The two couches faced one another around a small coffee table on the right, while a more formal desk and two chairs sat directly opposite the door. It was spacious with a large viewer screen on one wall, currently showing a fake city view.

To the left, pushed against the wall, was a substantial-looking assembly underneath a thick black cloth that reminded me of a...

Frowning, I walked over and lifted the cover up.

"No," I said, shaking my head. "No, that can't stay here." I snapped the cloth back down before stalking back through the waiting room and into the practice manager's office.

"How are the rooms?" Cora asked, smiling.

"There's a—" I gestured in the general direction of my office. "There's a...chair in the room," I said, which didn't make much sense because clearly, every room had chairs.

She frowned.

"A chair with stirrups. Did someone forget to remove it?"

"Ah," she said, shaking her head. "No. I don't believe so."

"It can't stay in the room."

"It's very heavy," she said reasonably. "Your room was a gynecologist's office. I'm afraid there's nothing we can do." She smiled. "This is only temporary, Abby. A week, two at the most, I was told. It was very inconvenient for them to take it out and then put it back in again. The gynecologist is on holiday, so they offered to leave it there."

"Goodness," I said inadequately.

"I'm sure nobody will know," she said. "You can barely notice it against those lime green walls."

I'd guessed what was underneath thirty seconds after entering the room.

My first client of the day arrived and brought the discussion to a close. When the young alpha spent more time staring not very subtly at the chair rather than me, I knew it would be a long day.

Kade

"Kevin," I muttered as we took the elevator up to the consulting rooms, where we would soon see Abby. "I can't believe that gecko loving bastard called me Kevin. Where the fuck did he get Kevin from?"

Jordan shrugged his shoulders, but I saw the way his lips were twitching as he fought a smile. He didn't smile very often and was a miserable bastard at the best of times. "There are worse names than Kevin," he said. "Besides, it doesn't fucking matter."

"Do you reckon she's going to call security?" I asked, suddenly nervous. Not about the security, which I was confident we could handle, but we'd learned a lot about Abby in the time between the space station attack and now.

Abby was a therapist from a wealthy theta family and dedicated her career to helping troubled people deal with stress. She had several papers to her name. I'd barely scraped through the mandatory schooling, which meant much of it went over my head, but it was clear that Abby was a pacifist at heart and lived a squeaky-clean life.

"No," he said.

"You sound confident," I said.

"I am," he replied. "There's no way she's gonna call security."

"She filed a restraining order."

"So she did." His grin was the feral one that could put the fear of god into regular people and gave even me cause to pause.

"So, no security," I said. "I don't think she's going to be happy, though."

"That goes without saying," he said. "She doesn't even know we're on Chimera, so I'd say it's gonna be a surprise."

"What if she doesn't want to see us?" I asked quietly as the numbers ticked up.

"It doesn't matter," he said.

"How can it not matter? You don't think she will freak out

about us breaking the terms of the restraining order? What about us being semi-criminals?"

He raised a brow. "Last night, we beat the shit out of three drug dealers we caught in Lucian's club and tossed their broken bodies in a dumpster."

He made a compelling point. "Okay, full criminals," I amended.

"She'll want to see us afterward," he said. "She just doesn't know us yet."

Then the elevator opened, and we were directed into a psychedelic waiting room.

I looked at Jordan. He looked at me and shrugged.

We sat in the sky blue chairs that were weirdly reclining and very fucking uncomfortable, staring at the hot pink walls and orange lava lamp, and waited.

Abby

"Your next appointment is here," my assistant messaged me.

"Wonderful," I replied.

They were a little early, but that wasn't a problem. I quickly pulled up the information on my data tablet and re-familiarized myself. James and Kevin were a couple looking for help with anger management, which was fine. They were both orphans who had come through the system. They must have done well for themselves. My services certainly weren't cheap, although the pricing was set by my consulting company and not me.

I liked that they came as a couple, though I sometimes preferred to see a client on their own. It was good to get a double perspective on things. It wasn't always the case, but often, I found it bode well for their relationship and willingness to change when they first came together.

We'd see how this session would go, and after, I could better judge and recommend some next steps. I enjoyed meeting new clients, learning about them and understanding their issues before forming a plan with them. I pushed my glasses up my nose and opened the file, ready to enter my notes.

Everything was in order. I went to the office door, and with a professional smile in place, opened it.

Only two men were in the waiting room, dressed entirely in black and looking awkward on the sky blue reception chairs.

"James and Kevin?" I asked slowly.

Their heads swung my way, and they jumped to their feet.

I frowned, looked around the waiting room, and then back at the two enormous deltas.

They took a collective step forward.

I stepped back.

"No," I said, shaking my head slowly, heart rate rocketing and vision coming through a tunnel. My traitorous pussy performed a slow clench as if to welcome them home.

No.

They looked between each other and then back at me.

"Oh god," I muttered weakly. "You're not Kevin and James, are you?" This wasn't happening. This couldn't possibly be real. How? Why?

"We're here for therapy."

Kade—aka Kevin, I was guessing—gave me a winning smile.

"Let's get her in the room," Jordan—aka James—said.

"There is monitoring in this area," I said as he took my arm and directed me into the room and shut the door.

"I know," he said. "Don't worry, we've dealt with it."

"You've—" I batted Jordan's hand off my arm and scowled at him. "What do you mean you've dealt with it?"

"Ah, buddy," Kade said. "You've got that eye-twitching thing going. You're scaring the little gamma. Take it down a notch."

Jordan, James, whatever the hell his name was, heaved a breath. The man was quivering.

"Why don't we sit down?" Kade said, putting himself between Jordan and me and indicating the couches.

"I don't want to sit down. I want you to leave immediately. I have a restraining order, for goodness' sake. You can't be here."

I was talking, but my feet were moving because Kade or Kevin was walking me in a gentle coaxing way, my hand clasped within his, toward the couch, where he sat me down before taking the seat opposite. My legs were as limp as cooked noodles, and I couldn't have stood up if my life depended on it. My life might actually depend on it!

My hands were shaking. In fact, the whole of me shook as the two deltas filled the opposite couch.

"We're here for therapy," Kade said. "Also, the restraining order. That's under Kade, and today, I'm Kevin." He said this all so reasonably, it was enough to make my head spin.

"Are you two deranged?" I hissed.

He smirked and nudged Jordan. "Probably," he said. "I've got a lot of issues to work through. That's why we're here."

Jordan growled. My head swung his way, but he wasn't staring at me. He was staring over my shoulder at that damned gynecologist chair that didn't look like anything but a gynecologist chair poorly disguised under a cloth covering.

I shook my head, trying to find my wits, and ignored how my entire body had come alive because I didn't need any distraction. "I don't care what name you use," I muttered. "How do you even have another name?"

"Why don't you ask us about our childhood?" Kade asked,

nodding toward my data tablet resting on the coffee table between us. "I've got lots to say."

"You're not listening to a word I say."

"I thought it was the other way around," Kade said, frowning. "I thought you asked us questions, and then listened to us."

"Yes, yes, that's how therapy usually works, but this isn't therapy, is it?"

"It's therapy," Jordan said. They were the first words he'd uttered since he'd put his hands on me. His touch had been light, but I could still feel the warmth of where his hand had been.

My mind decided to bombard me with images from the last time we'd been together. I swallowed, then picked up my data tablet.

Play along, Abby, I said to myself. *You can do this. Get through the session. They're not doing anything threatening.* Other than Jordan's growling, which had eased off now as his gaze moved toward the tablet in my hands.

"That color is very pretty on you," Kade said. "It matches your eyes."

Heaven help me, I needed to pull myself together. "Thank you," I said, plastering on a professional smile again. "But if you're here for therapy, let's get to it."

"Great," Kade said, relaxing back into his seat.

I blinked a few times and had to remind myself to breathe when the relaxed pose stretched the material of his shirt across a wall of hard muscle. Had he always been that huge? Had he gotten bigger?

I was staring at him. The breadth of his shoulders, the way he filled out that black shirt, and those muscular thighs, parted... Fuck! Now I was staring at his crotch!

I snapped my eyes back to the data tablet. No, I could not

see him smirking out of the corner of my eye. I wasn't going to acknowledge that.

"So," I said, tapping *FOCUS!!!* at the top of my data tablet screen. "Why don't you tell me what brought you here? Let's start with you, Kade."

Somehow, and despite my initial shock, we got through the therapy session easier than I'd have thought. They sat on their couch, and I sat on mine, with a hot purple coffee table between us, surrounded by lime green walls...and near that damn gynecologist chair that Jordan couldn't stop looking at.

They talked, and I took notes, and truthfully, despite my fears, it went about how a regular therapy session might go with new clients. Mostly, Kade did the talking, but Jordan occasionally grunted something. I got the impression I was receiving a sanitized version of events, but that wasn't unusual in a first session.

It turned out they worked for a businessman here in Chimera as private security. Not only were they on the same planet as me, but in the same city. What were the chances within all the habitable planets of the Empire? The one place I least should have gone, and I'd just come here.

Only they were nothing like I'd expected. While I still suspected they had ulterior motives in visiting me specifically, I went through the motions of therapy.

As the session ended, Kade asked me earnestly if they could book one for next week.

Jordan stared at me with a brooding expression, like he was remembering me on my knees with his cock down my throat.

I said yes. I told myself I was saying yes now so I could get them out the door, then I would cancel it and tell security not to let them in again.

Only as the door clicked shut and I was alone, because they were the last appointments of my day, I wondered, what was the harm?

Maybe they really did need therapy. I sensed they carried scars and that I might even be able to help them.

Jordan, the one who had said the least and who'd given the reason for this therapy, called to my instinctive empathy.

We were all dancing around the main issue, though; that they wanted me, and I wanted them.

Was this them getting to know me? Was this a soft approach that everybody said the deltas weren't capable of?

They didn't come with an opt-out clause—everybody I'd talked to and everything I'd read suggested as much. Yet here I was, and here they were, and I was so curious.

As I shifted in my chair, the unmistakable dampness between my thighs forced me to acknowledge that I was also aroused. God, there was just so much of them. It took concerted effort to maintain eye contact to keep my focus on their faces or my data tablet, when I was so aware of them. Had I sounded a little breathless at times? I thought that I had.

After they left, I checked my calendar, and there it was, next week—another appointment with them at the same time, same day. I ought to decline it, but I didn't.

I'd seen them once. We'd sat down and been civilized. Was there any harm in seeing them again?

I might be a therapist and a psychologist, yet it was hard to be objective when it pertained to yourself. I just kept thinking about how I felt when I was between them.

My hands trembled as I closed up my data tablet and slipped it into the slot on my desk. I left the appointment there. I could cancel it tomorrow.

Only I didn't cancel it tomorrow, nor the day after. Nor the day after that.

My books were full, and my days were busy.

I saw them three more times, and with each session, I felt that heightened awareness between us.

It was only after I went to collect my coffee as per usual, precisely one month later, that I realized my mistake.

Chapter Twelve

Abby

As I opened my office door, I could practically smell the testosterone, which was impressive, given I was a gamma and had the worst sense of smell.

I looked between Jordan, Kade, and Ryker and sighed. I must have been asleep to allow appointments with them back-to-back. We were still renovating my original offices. The two-week estimate had blown out to two months, due to interruptions with supplies. My temporary office was already giving me a headache from the color scheme, never mind that the former gynecologist's consulting room still hosted a poorly covered examination chair.

Every time I broached the topic of getting it removed with the efficient beta office manager, she gave me the runaround.

Ryker, complete with military casuals and a black eye, was sprawled in a neon pink chair beside a luminous orange lava lamp. The combination of Ryker in a pink chair under the glow of an orange table lamp made my eyes twitch.

God, he'd actually asked me if I wanted him to get rid of Jordan and Kade back on Tolis. I'd have liked to think he'd been joking, but you never really knew with Ryker.

He smirked like he could read my mind. Kade and Jordan leaped to their feet. Jordan's eye was twitching , and Kade was growling.

This morning, when I'd asked where the regular barista had gone and the replacement informed me that my boyfriends had been around, I'd seen red and canceled their appointment.

"Ryker is next," I said, pushing my glasses up my nose. I knew Ryker's smirk all too well and had no doubt he'd been taunting Jordan and Kade in some way. For once, I thought he might be biting off more than he could handle with the two deltas. If they didn't like a barista being polite to me, goodness only knew what they would do to a much more tangible threat.

Then there was Ryker, who would only meet such a challenge with equal and opposite force. He was also a psychopath with a propensity for chaos, who had recently been allocated joint controller status for Lillian Brach. I was confident the only reason he'd avoided a stint in a military prison was because his father was a high-ranking general who found ways to sweep his antics under the rug.

I had a mental picture of a bomb crater with a small inadequate Persian rug over it, and every time I got another report of Ryker's misadventures, the rug to crater ratio diminished.

Usually, it was Jordan who worried me the most, but today, Kade's chest was heaving like an angry bull about to charge. I wondered which one of them had had 'words' with the male beta, whose only crime was to smile and sneak me a cookie.

Ryker prowled over with a chipper smile on his face. "No prize for guessing who's on top," he said.

Both Jordan and Kade growled.

"Ryker!" I snapped.

Ryker chuckled, because he lived to bait people and couldn't help himself. That I had responded to his antics would make his day. I should have had my second coffee. I needed to fire on all cylinders today.

"No need to get all growly, guys," Ryker continued in that overly cheerful tone. "I'm actually here for therapy."

I took a deep breath as Ryker strode past me into the room. "Ryker, we've spoken about this before," I said, retrieving my data tablet and taking one of the poppy red couches opposite the fake window viewer that displayed Chimera's cityscape. I could almost ignore the lime green walls if I faced this direction.

I began tapping my update into the data tablet as Ryker took his merry time, wondering if I should call security on Jordan and Kade or bluff my way through a therapy session one more time.

Ryker was staring at the poorly disguised gynecologist's chair, *again*. I'd left him alone for five minutes when an urgent call came through during the last session here, and I was sure the nosy alpha looked underneath.

Nobody could take their damn eyes off it.

I pointed at the couch opposite when he didn't immediately sit, then did a double take. Up close, the black eye was making me feel a little queasy. "What...happened to you?" I asked, pushing my glasses up my nose again. Had Kade actually thumped him in my reception room?

"I'm disappointed in you not noticing Ethan's welcome home gift sooner," Ryker said, going straight into asshole mode. I could already tell the two deltas had stirred the pot with Ryker, and it was going to be a testing day. At least it wasn't Kade who had punched him. Still, Ethan was the second controller allocated to Lilly, and I was now concerned about that. Not for Ryker, who I was sure could hold his own, and further, if he'd been punched, he probably deserved it, but for Lilly.

"I guess the deltas weren't the only ones distracted." His eyes drifted toward the examination chair again like it was painted with a target.

My lips tightened, and my knuckles turned white around the data tablet. After three years, I was on to all his tricks, so why was I letting him get to me today? "Would you like to issue a complaint?"

"Complaint?" His brows crawled into his hairline. "Against Ethan? Fuck no, I don't want to issue a complaint. I had the best blowjob of my life because of these injuries. I should be thanking him!"

Nope, I was not rising to that. "Fine then, tell me about your last operation," I said.

"You know they want to fuck you, right?" he asked, because this was Ryker and he made it his mission to waste as much of his thirty-minute slot as possible. "Both of them, because deltas do everything in twos."

"Was that you requesting to talk about your mother, Ryker?" I asked sweetly, tapping away on my tablet with more vigor than was strictly professional. He was asking very personal questions, which was both inappropriate and a red flag. It was hard to say sometimes with Ryker whether he was just being playfully obtuse or real-life issues were bothering him. Still, the report of him being allocated as a controller to Lilly, along with Ethan, might also be behind this. Unlike deltas, alphas did not like to share.

"Nope, don't think I was," he said reasonably before stabbing his thumb in the direction of the door. "Do you want me to give them a bit of a thumping for you? See how serious they are about this pursuit?"

"No, thank you, Ryker." I needed to ask the practice to

bring my rates up. "You have an unauthorized weapon use infringement listed against you during the Tolis operation. A" —I paused to squint at my data tablet— "rocket-propelled grenade launcher was fired eight times without the relevant ticket."

"I had the ticket," he said.

"No." I shook my head, indicating the tablet. "Your license ticket was revoked after a prior operation where" —I paused again to read the poorly written report— "a food service tent was accidentally destroyed."

Ryker winced. "Accident? You're my therapist, Abby, so I know I can be candid and it won't go any further." He pointed at the tablet. "That's just command covering up my antics, because it can get very exhausting dealing with them and I'm useful the rest of the time, but I definitely meant to destroy it. Got a cheer for my effort from the troops based there. If you'd eaten the food they were serving, you'd have cheered me on too."

"I very much doubt it," I said with bite. "Your allocation to this omega appears to have made quite an impression."

For the briefest moment, his playful façade dropped. "I think I'm addicted," he said in way that sounded unusually honest.

"Doctor Brach has had a challenging time. I'm not convinced you're the best choice," I said, frowning. "Are you remembering to follow all my instructions on omega care?"

When he didn't answer immediately, I paused my notes to pin him with a look.

"Yes," he said, wary eyes shifting between me and the pad in my hand.

A noticeable and lengthy silence followed, one I was determined not to fill, letting him sweat it out, because he knew I had sway and that a one-word answer was not sufficient in this case.

"I make the sounds," he said at length.

I blinked a couple of times as that sank in. He was clearly very attached to Lilly. *Addicted* was his choice of word, and a telling one. He lived a very polarized existence, and other than blowing up a food service tent, had been part of numerous high-profile military operations. He lived right up to the line, though, one I had coached him on at length. "Ryker, I've been your therapist for three years, and I only want the best outcome for you... I wish I could stay to guide you through what will undoubtedly be a difficult period."

I'd probably regret letting that slip, but after the incident with the barista, I'd decided to leave. Sure, it would take time to get everything in order.

"Where are you going?" There was a definite note of panic in his voice. This might be the most vulnerable Ryker had been in his life.

"I've taken a position...on an orbital station," I said, which was a ridiculous lie, given I'd come very close to dying on an orbital space station a short time ago and would have to be mad to go to one again. Still, I was mindful of the two deltas waiting outside, plus the fewer people who knew exactly where the job was, the better.

Also, I hadn't technically taken the position, but the offer had come out of the blue two days ago. The package and opportunity were even better than I was getting here.

It was a chance to escape.

Did I want to escape?

"If you're trying to escape their pursuit, it won't work," Ryker said like he could read my damn mind, gesturing at me and then over my shoulder toward the door. "Dark and brooding was ready to rip my head off, and all I did was sit down. Deltas are like sharks locked in on a blood trail once they set their sights on a gamma."

"Ryker! The line!" I'd thought Lilly had put it bluntly, but Ryker managed to take it up another notch. And yes, I was very much sensing that they were indeed locked on to me.

"Sorry." He rubbed the back of his head. "You know you're going to miss me. Can we do the therapy via transmitter? I might go AWOL if you're not here to remind me about the line."

My lips twitched because Ryker, despite his numerous personality disorders, was hard to be cross with. "I'll see what I can do."

The rest of the session went reasonably well. We discussed omega care in further detail, and he satisfied me that he would follow the rules regarding this at least.

By the time we were done and I was walking him to the door, I'd been fooled into thinking he was behaving.

I should have known better by now.

He cracked his knuckles as he exited my office and called out, "Might need to get those restraint straps repaired before your next client."

Kade

It had been a shitty week. We'd been to the docks twice more and gotten into a fight on both occasions. One of my ribs was cracked, and my shoulder was aching like a bastard. My knuckles were sore, and my right hand was bruised. Jordan hadn't fared much better, with a faint discoloration along his jaw, visible if anybody looked too closely.

Lucien wasn't happy that the next shipment hadn't come

through yet, but some things were beyond our control. To make matters worse, our other boss, the one with all the power, was also demanding answers. He had skin in the game too, although he was more interested in the Uncorrupted's plans, not that we had any answers on that. We didn't have answers on anything.

But we were seeing Abby today.

Jordan had fucked me raw last night, and I'd accepted every depraved moment with joy because we'd both needed something to take the edge off before seeing Abby. It was getting harder and harder to keep our hands off the little gamma, especially after the guy we'd had tailing her reported some beta prick barista checking out her ass.

That ass belonged to us, and I'd rearrange any fucker who thought otherwise.

I was normally the chill one, but we were both edgy, and this before the alpha bastard in Abby's reception had given us an eyeballing. When her office door finally opened and Ryker stalked out, I growled at him with all the finesse of an angry bull.

It was only the Gecko screaming in my earpiece not to start a fucking fight in the reception room, because he had no access to override the surveillance there, keeping me in check. We hustled her into the office in double time and slammed the door shut.

"Tell me it's fucking clear," Jordan snarled into the communicator.

"*It's clear,*" the Gecko said.

"What? What are you doing?" Abby asked, looking between us with a frown, but also breathless in a way that made my cock sit up and say hello.

Then there was her fucking dress. Every one of them drove me fucking nuts. I'd never seen a woman in such a shapeless piece of clothing in all my life, yet thoughts of the sexy under-wear underneath sent blood pounding south.

Jordan turned without a word and slipped the lock into place. It was probably meant for patients when they were being... Damn, that fucking chair.

"We need to breed her," I said, the words tumbling out of my mouth. I swear I was in some sort of trance.

"Breed? No, absolutely not. Unlock the door!" Abby planted her small fists on her hips and scowled at us over the rim of her glasses.

Yeah, that wasn't going to work today. I plucked the glasses from her nose and put them on her desk.

"I can't see! Now you're both just a big blur," she wailed. "Really, this doesn't help. Give me my glasses and unlock my door!"

"No can do, sweetheart," I said. "That's not happening, and I don't want to get them damaged."

"Damaged? This is outrageous. Open the door at once."

The door wasn't opening, and as I stepped into her, Jordan rounded and stepped into her back, pinning her between us, right where she belonged. I looked down, a long way down because she was tiny, and her breath hitched. I tucked her short hair behind her ear.

"You're so fucking beautiful," I said. "All I thought about all week was getting inside you again."

Her mouth opened and closed again. She blinked several times. Her eyes had that unfocused look. I guessed she really couldn't see. No matter. She didn't need to see anything for what we had planned. My fingers trailed down her cheek, and I settled them at the base of her throat. I stepped into her, but she took a half step back, then gasped as she bumped into Jordan.

His hand settled on my shoulders. "Perfect," he said.

"Agreed," I said.

My world narrowed to the tiny woman standing in front of me. I became aware of her on a thousand different and incredibly nuanced levels, from her blown pupils and the slight hitch in her breaths, to the way her pulse thumped underneath my thumb as her tongue darted out to lick her dry lips.

She wanted this—no, she *needed* this.

I picked her up, Jordan instinctively moving with me, clamping his hand around her waist.

"What are you doing? Oh!"

Squishing her perfectly between us, I closed my mouth over hers, one arm under her ass, encouraging her legs to open around my waist. Her lips parted, and I plundered, tongue exploring the sweet cavern of her mouth as we shared a kiss.

Her moan, low and needy, told me she was all-in. My dick, kicked against my zipper, impatient to get inside her, and to hook her again. I'd fill her hot pussy the way she needed, jetting my cum inside, *breeding* her, because I needed her linked irrevocably to us, where she belonged.

Savage instincts were running riot. I remembered how we had discussed her, decided we would take it slow, be patient, and show her we could be civilized for her.

This wasn't slow nor patient. This was a nuclear explosion inside my head and an unquenchable need to claim her.

I couldn't give a fuck about time. The little gamma was all out of luck.

Jordan's hands were underneath, lifting the hem of her grim dress up and out of the way. A distinct tearing noise followed, but I kept her occupied with my tongue down her throat, and whatever protest she might have voiced was lost as I deepened the kiss.

A *chink* followed. This time, it wasn't me who would be getting my cock in her, but Jordan.

She tore her lips from mine and glanced over her shoulder,

then all the air ejected from her lungs as Jordan lined up and thrust.

Her squeak was high and not entirely pleasure, but on the second thrust she moaned, and a flush stained her pretty cheeks.

"Fuck, she feels good," Jordan rumbled, hands on her hips as he began to power into her, crushing her between us.

"Hush," I said, cupping her hot cheeks and turning her face back toward me. "Let him have this, Abby. He didn't get to hook you last time, and he needs this."

She groaned. "God, please hurry."

Fuck yes! I kissed up her words as she clung to me, her small hands grasping my neck as Jordan fucked up into her from behind. If I felt savage, it was fair to say that Jordan was more so.

When I lifted my head, I saw what he was doing—marking her, sucking hard against her throat.

"Yes," I said, voice low and rough. "Mark up what's ours." Distantly, I recognized I was getting ahead of myself, but I didn't fucking care. I cupped her face with one hand, the other holding her up, watching all the emotions play out, kissing the corners of her mouth, her hot cheeks, and her temple while she gasped, groaned, and sometimes squealed.

"I can't, I can't," she mumbled.

"You can, sweetheart," I said. "You definitely can. You took my hook already. You can do it again for Jordan. Relax, hmm, that's it. Just trust us to take care of you."

"Relax?" she said. "I... Oh god, how?"

"I need better leverage," Jordan said with a grunt, stilling.

"The chair?" I asked.

"Not the chair," Abby said.

"Definitely the chair," Jordan countered.

We had the cover off, her dress off, and her ass in the chair.

Jordan had already torn through her pink lace panties, and she wore only the shreds and a matching bra.

I palmed her throat to keep her good and still as Jordan got her legs in the stirrups and a couple of handy Velcro fasteners in place.

"You can't be serious—Oh god!"

Jordan growled, slamming deep and holding. I swear there was no blood in my brain to process how this looked because it was all in my dick. Little gamma was all spread out and trussed up, taking a deep fucking.

"Fucking perfect," Jordan said, reaching down to strum her clit.

A jolt went through her. She danced her ass around on the chair until he pinned her still and worked her clit without mercy, taking her deep and hard, and chasing the deepest, most depraved, most savage penetration.

I palmed her tit, pinching a nipple through her bra and eliciting a sharp squeal from her lips.

"Keep doing that," Jordan said. "Makes her squeeze so good around my cock."

I ripped her bra cup down, closed my mouth over her nipple, and sucked hard. She arched up, trying to buck us off, moaning wildly, hands trying to fucking scalp me.

Abby

Here I was, on the chair, that damn gynecologist's chair, the bane of my existence since I'd moved into this office. Where had it gone wrong? I tried to process how I'd gotten from them entering my room to being strapped down and filled, but the steps between were lost under a haze. Every nerve in my body tingled, my pussy fluttering on the brink of a climax, my senses overflowing with the two men who worked my body in ways I didn't know I needed and would argue that I couldn't take.

Yet take it, I did.

Kade's hair was soft under my fingers, his lips on my breast creating a tingly urgency that fell into perfect synchronicity with the rising euphoria as Jordan filled me with his cock.

Emotions rushed through me with every pounding thrust and drugging pull of Kade's lips. I was right where I was supposed to be, only heaven help me, I was still terrified of the hook.

Jordan

I lost myself the moment I entered her room and locked the door. A deep-rooted imperative demanded I stake my claim. This chair was fucking perfect—heavy enough that it didn't move an inch, no matter how hard I pounded against it. I would get something just like it as soon as I was done here.

Only I wasn't close to being done.

Her hot cunt gushing and squeezing over me lit explosions in my brain, and I stroked into her deeply like I was trying to become one with her.

Kade continued to tease her tits, sucking on one as he mauled the other, making her gasp and clench, which was a fucking delight around my cock.

Her hooded eyes implored me for mercy.

Unfortunately for our little gamma, I had none, not while she was half mindless on pleasure. I liked that—being in control, driving her higher toward the edge of that cliff. I'd had the best blowjob of my life watching Kade fuck her from behind. His pleasure, her pleasure, and mine melded into one perfect erotic storm.

My hook began to tingle, wanting in, demanding I deliver what was needed. With her legs spread wide and high, I had the perfect angle for me to penetrate the entrance to her womb and seek the ultimate prize.

"Come for me, Abby," I commanded, thumb swiping over her fat, slippery clit with every stroke. "Come all over my cock, and I'm going to fill you how you need."

"Oh god, oh god, oh god," she chanted. "I can't."

"You can, baby," Kade said, palming her throat, lips trailing kisses over her hot cheeks. "Open for him."

The tip of my cock was tingling, changing, swelling, and rising. The thick bulbous head would be elongating, narrowing to a tapered tip, ridged layers unfurling in anticipation of the breech.

"Fuck, Fuck, Fuck," I muttered. Sensing my need, Kade slipped his fingers down to pet her slick clit so I could take her hips in my hands.

***

Abby

I knew what was coming, and it was messing with my mind. The pressure building inside me had me teetering on the cusp of madness. I wanted to come, sensed I was close, but as Jordan took my hips in his hands and began to power into me, the dark, twisted pleasure came for me again.

I couldn't breathe. The air seemed to trap in my lungs as I hung suspended out of time. Jordan's growling grunts as he took me filled my ears, along with the heavy pounding of my own blood.

I wasn't in my body anymore. I looked down on myself from above, sprawled out lewdly on my back, with two huge males over me, playing with me, lifting me impossibly higher.

Then I rushed back, a squeal tearing from my lips as I was penetrated in the deepest, darkest ways. The pain momentarily robbed me of breath and thought before my body tumbled over into wave after wave of bliss. My back arched off the chair, and my whole body turned rigid.

Jordan slammed deep and stilled, and I stared at him, mouth hanging open on a cry of pure ecstasy. Deep inside came the strange tickling sensation, like tiny sinuous fingers skittering over my most intimate place, *caressing* me. God, was that his hook? I had a strange sensation of tentacle-like protrusions—but that couldn't possibly be—opening me up, stretching me...and then a hot, heavy flood.

Jordan

I growled lowly, fingers tightening on her hips.

"Good girl," Kade said. "Such a good girl for us.

I wanted to memorize her face, the shock followed by the rapture, as she jerked and twitched and came all over me, encouraging me deeper, milking the cum from my tightly drawn balls. I was coming, she was coming, and neither of us could stop. Locked together as we were, thoroughly hooked, there was no escaping this until I'd drained every fucking drop.

My hands were shaking, and I could feel Abby trembling uncontrollably beneath them.

Cum was leaking out, spilling over my balls, and dripping onto the floor. Kade kissed her, swallowing up her groans. Deep inside her, my cock flexed, and her pussy fluttered in response, pulling hot and tight around me.

"Tell me that feels good," Kade demanded.

"Oh god." She groaned.

"It does, doesn't it," Kade said, lips hovering over hers. "Is Jordan filling you up good?"

"Yes, yes, yes!" She jerked, chasing his lips when he moved them away until he relented and gave her his mouth.

Her pussy tightened over my cock, my balls tightened to the point of pain, and I ejected another small but heady gush of cum. This right here was the only heaven I needed.

Little gamma might need to catch up, because as far as I was concerned, she was already ours.

Abby

As experiences went, I'd thought the hot sex that followed the space station attack had been the wildest of my life.

Kade hadn't even got his cookie, and I was confident today had already left the previous encounter for dust.

My legs were freed, then Jordan, still deeply hooked, lifted me from the gynecologist's chair. He shuffled over to the couch and dropped into the seat with me clinging to him like a monkey, trembling and still coming in tight little spasms and not entirely mentally present.

I felt like I'd been broken.

I also felt like I was whole.

Not quite whole, though, as the big body knelt between Jordan's legs and pressed against my back wasn't yet inside me. I wanted him to be, wanted him with a desperation that shook me. His hands skimmed over my body as I buried my face against Jordan's chest.

"Fuck," Kade said gruffly, lips trailing over my shoulder and leaving a trail of goose bumps. "I need inside her. Are you going to let me in, sweetheart?"

Kade's hands paused at my hips, and I dragged my nose from Jordan's chest to look back at him. My pussy clenched, and my breath hitched as I blinked at the unfocused version of him. I didn't need to see him. I could sense his desperation in the faint tremble of his hands. My body had always attracted attention before I'd learned to cover it. For once, and although they clearly enjoyed my body, I felt like they wanted *me*, the inner me, the part that was a gamma, and who was the perfect fit for them.

"I can't see you without my glasses," I said, my voice carrying that needy whine because I wanted him inside me, but I couldn't work out how to take him when I was already so full —beyond full. I felt like I was joined with Jordan, like he was inside me...in ways no other male could.

"You don't need your glasses," Jordan said, redirecting my attention to him. He held my eyes, his handsome face blurred before his head lowered, and I knew he was staring at my breasts. He cupped them together and issued a filthy growl that made me clench around his hard length, then he groaned, cock flexing inside me.

Distantly, I knew I was about to take a step from which there would be no return.

A faint buzzing came from the direction of Jordan's watch. He muttered a curse and tightened his arms around me. "See what he wants," he said to Kade.

Kade heaved himself up, the buzzing continuing as he moved to the other side of the room.

I already sensed what was coming, even before he said the words.

"We need to go?"

"Now?" Jordan asked.

"Yeah now," Kade said, sounding as disappointed as I was. "It's going down tonight, and we need to be there."

"I'm sorry, baby," Jordan said, cupping my cheek, and thumb brushing over my swollen lips before he lowered his mouth over mine.

"It's okay," I replied, only it wasn't okay, and I didn't want them to go. I wanted to ask what was going down because something in the phrase made me very uneasy. Only they weren't my business, not yet. Soon, I hoped they would be, that I could ask them and they would tell me.

One thing was sure—I couldn't be their therapist anymore.

Chapter Thirteen

Jordan

After two intense days of chasing leads the breadth of Chimera, we finally had a tip-off on the package handover. Perhaps after this was sorted out, we'd have some time with Abby.

"I can't believe she canceled our next therapy session," Kade said as we loaded up into the skycar, our destination, once more, Chimera's central cargo docks.

"I can," I replied, not that I was going to let that stop us. Double fuck no.

Getting my hook into our gamma should have put me in a good mood.

It hadn't.

I was borderline feral.

We also had a job to do, and shit was going on beyond our personal lives that couldn't be avoided, which put claiming Abby on temporary hold.

Well, until tonight, because as soon as this shit was sorted out, we were breaking into her apartment and reminding a certain gamma that she was ours.

It wasn't a civilized approach, but one of the best things about being a delta was that people expected us to be savage. No point in disappointing them. Also, once we were mated, what was anyone going to do?

Nothing.

There hadn't been time nor space for mating Abby in her office, although I had to be honest with myself—it had been hard to leave for work demands after I'd taken her in that chair.

We definitely needed a proper bench for her in our home, because there was no doubt that strapping her down like that, all vulnerable like an offering, had been off the charts hot for all parties involved.

That was for later. First, we had a job that waited on no one.

We landed a couple of blocks away and walked the rest of the distance on foot.

Here, we met up with Ethan Black and Ryker Sherwin, two of Lucian's contacts with a vested interest in Sanders. We had orders from Lucian to retrieve the shipment. I'd met Ethan before. He had the same unofficial boss as us, so we'd occasionally crossed paths. He was a fucking massive alpha who looked like he could crush skulls with his bare hands. The military command used him in undercover ops, so it was fair to assume he had skills to back up the menacing vibe he had going on.

We'd met Ryker Sherwin exactly once. The information pack the Gecko had sent us to look over while in transit indicated he was a particularly crazy brand of psycho, which explained why he was seeing Abby.

Kade slugged him, and I winced. He'd been working out extra hard since our return from space, so I'd been on the receiving end of that fist in our sparring sessions. It hurt even when he pulled his punches.

"Fuck!" Ryker muttered, cupping his right eye, which was already watering and swelling. He'd been battered when we met in Abby's waiting room, and he didn't look much better today even before Kade's welcome punch. "The fuck do they feed you?"

Ethan raised a brow and looked between them. He didn't question Kade's action, and we didn't offer an explanation. The information pack had also mentioned that Black and Ryker were currently joint controllers of Lillian Branch.

That had to be messy. Hard to say whether the viral doctor or Ethan had drawn the short straw there.

Still, in our brief interaction with Ryker, he'd been annoying as fuck. If the Uncorrupted didn't kill him on a mission, there was a fair chance someone closer to home would end the fucker, which would sort the problem out.

"Is that the new super lightweight armor?" Ryker asked Kade, still squinting through his blackening eye. "I heard they were making it into civilian clothes."

"Yeah," Kade said, holding his arm out for inspection, all business now. "It'll stop a knife, no problem. We get a lot of action in our line of work."

"Yeah? Nice," Ryker said. "I heard Lucian has some sweet weapons in his..."

I tuned the rest out. Kade loved his fucking toys and could talk about them all day. Lucian didn't skimp on anything pertaining to security. His kit was quality.

Black nodded his head at security gates a short walk away. Ryker and Kade didn't stop talking the whole fucking time. When Black looked at me in question, I muttered, "Kids and their toys."

We passed security, where they checked us for weapons.

Dock security had been ramped up after an incident two years ago, and now it was so tight that not even Lucian had found a loophole. I felt fucking naked without a piece or a knife. If trouble kicked off, we'd have to deal with it the old-fashioned way.

It was evening, and although the docks worked nonstop, it was jam-packed with the seedy bars spilling noise and patrons onto the walkways.

"Just up ahead," I said to Black. "We've got a tag on the shipment handler, and he's in Reaper's Revenge."

I didn't know the full details of Black's involvement in this, but we all had the same objective—stop the handover and intercept the shipment. Lucian had two other teams inside the docks keeping tabs on the cargo, which sat in a container bay awaiting clearance.

Mikael Sanders officially worked for a transport company shipping legal supplies for the government viral program. Word was, he had an additional package destined for the Uncorrupted.

Black wanted Sanders.

Lucian wanted the package.

We came to a collective stop at the entrance.

Ryker grinned and muttered, "Fuck yeah!" Pushing open the door, he stalked in.

Reaper's Revenge, the dive bar from hell, was becoming more familiar than I might have preferred. The asshole bartender gave me a sour nod.

"How the fuck did you find somewhere with this much of a security nightmare?" Black asked, shoving a drunk dockworker aside.

"This is where it's supposed to happen," I said. "He hands over the security tag. The contact picks up the viral shipment from the holding pen and returns the tag to Mikael, who goes on about his business like it never happened."

We made our way to the bar and ordered drinks, getting a visual on Mikael, who sat in the corner, talking to a beta woman. "We're not the only eyes in here," Kade said.

We'd barely taken a sip of our drinks when Ryker put his back down. "They're on to us."

"Fuck, I think you're right," I said.

Behind us, three alphas had arrived, cutting off our exit. Ugly on the right held a disabler stick. Yeah, that fucker wasn't dock security, and he had no business with one. The shock turned whatever it touched numb, which was very inconvenient if you were fighting for your life.

"How the fuck did they get a disabler through security?" Kade asked.

"We're busted," Black said, all business. "Get a hold of Sanders." A chair swung for Ethan's head.

We both ducked. Ethan went in swinging. Blood splattered in a great arc...and a roar went up as patrons scrambled over and around the beaten furnishings, creating a chaotic jumble of flying fists and stampeding feet.

One of the alphas charged me. Kade's shoulder barged him, and I grabbed the bastard around the neck, getting a lock on him. It wasn't good enough to choke the big fucker out. The best I could do was keep him out of the fray as Kade wrestled another to the ground and Ryker dived for Sanders, who was beating a path for the exit.

"The fuck is going down here?" I snarled into my communicator.

"*You can't blame me for everything,*" the Gecko said. "*Don't let Sanders get out. We won't get another shot at this!*"

Ryker was on the floor, grappling with Sanders. Two more men piled on top of him, creating one great mele. I was still trying to choke the alpha I had in a headlock and finally resorted to beating his head into the bar. Meanwhile, Black was using a chair to smack the shit out of anyone who came near.

The alpha in my lock finally went limp after the third battering of his head against the bar. A bottle smashed over my head. I winded my attacker with an elbow to the gut before kicking his legs out just as the wail of approaching sirens cut through the screams, shouts, growls, and snarls.

I staggered toward Ryker, still grappling with Sanders on the floor and getting a pounding by two alpha goons.

Another alpha went to charge in, but I lowered my head and tackled him to the ground, just as Black strode over and kicked one of the men on Ryker away.

"*Security are on their way,*" the Gecko said. "*You need to get the tag, now, and get the fuck out of there.*"

No shit! The sirens were getting louder.

The fight on the floor was far from over.

It took all three of us to get a lock on the thick-necked alpha still on Ryker and rip the fucker away.

Several more punches later, the big bastard finally went down.

This smelled a lot like a setup.

The wail drowned out the patrons' screams. If anyone had made it out during the brawl, I couldn't tell.

"We need to fucking leave," I called, snatching up a bottle and smashing it over another of Sanders' buddies trying to wade in.

The crowd, whipped into a frenzy, most of them probably in possession of something illegal, were as eager to escape as us and surged forward with renewed vigor, taking Sanders with them.

I tried to grab him, just as security pushed in and set about zapping anyone and everyone they could reach with their disabler rods. I kicked the fucker in the nuts. He sank to his knees with a grunt.

Ryker was still on the floor, trapped. Black and I grabbed an arm, and with Kade running interference on the heavy-handed security, we stumbled out the back just as more guards turned up.

"A fucking a setup," I snarled into my communicator. "This is the last fucking game you play, you gecko loving prick. I'm going to rip your fucking heart out and feed it to the ducks."

"*Ducks?*" the Gecko muttered. "*Really, the ducks? Do you think that works contextually with ripping a heart out?*"

Black was growling some shit at me, but I didn't hear a word.

"You and your sick fucking games," I snarled, pacing, about to lose my shit. "I'm going to break your geek ass, and I'm going to feed that to the ducks as well."

"*Oh, I'm so fucking scared. Why don't you grow some brain cells, then we can have a civilized conversation about how this is not my fucking fault.*"

"Later, asshole, I am going to find you."

I snapped my communicator off, chest heaving, and finally looked around as more security barged past us into the bar.

Ryker looked like he'd been through a one-man war, was bleeding heavily from his cheek and nose, and had an impressive egg forming on his temple, along with the prior black eye from Kade. His bloodstained teeth, when he grinned was grim.

"Fuck knows how you stay so pretty," Black muttered, shaking his head. "Please tell me you got the security tag?"

Ryker's grin turned smug, and he opened his palm to reveal the tag.

"Thank fuck," Black said. "Let's go and check if all this pain was for nothing."

It wasn't. We found the omega drug waiting in the cold

compartment, as we'd been tipped off. A quick check with the lab kit I had in my pocket, which had miraculously survived the brawl, confirmed this.

We had the shipment, but Sanders had gotten away.

"Tell Lucian to put a watch on Sanders," Black said. "If he pokes his head up somewhere I can get to him, I want to know."

Chapter Fourteen

Abby

I t was fair to say that life in my office was never quite the same after the infamous gynecologist chair moment. I'd been uncomfortable around it before, but now, heat blazed in my cheeks and I felt an involuntary and embarrassing clench low in my belly every time I walked into the office... every time I glanced at it...every time a client looked over and saw it. So, yeah, pretty much all day long, from the moment I opened the office door until I closed it again at the end of the day.

Then there were the dreams.

As if my feelings toward Jordan and Kade weren't confused enough, one of my colleagues mentioned that the supposedly nice barista had been fired. He'd been caught getting a blowjob from a customer in the stock room. Apparently, it wasn't the first time.

I canceled Jordan and Kade's next therapy session, but not

because I was mad. I still wanted to see them, desperately, only not in a fake therapy session.

I expected them to get in contact.

They didn't, and it felt strangely presumptuous to make the first move.

I was still wallowing in confusion as to what next when my parents insisted, in that gentle but firm way of theirs, that I visit them for dinner.

I didn't want dinner with my parents. What I wanted was hot sex with two delta men, the missing part of me.

I knew what was coming with Jordan and Kade. We had been building up to it slowly. I was ready to mate with them, wanted it, even though I had no idea how to broach the subject of me taking not just one mate, but two, with my parents. Then, and supposing I could get them past unsavory words like *mating*, there was Jordan and Kade with their rough accents and work as private security. It wasn't exactly an occupation my parents could relate to.

I couldn't relate to their work myself, and nor had they elaborated on it during therapy. Mainly, we'd discussed Jordan's anger management issues. There was no doubt the man was complex, but I'd long since surmised that they had only sought therapy to facilitate our relationship.

I wasn't even mad about it.

Given time, I thought my parents would come around, and if they didn't, I would deal with that too. When it came down to it, my feelings for them were too great to be ignored.

It was strange how only now I recognized the half-life I'd been living. Finally, I'd found my missing pieces in the most unexpected circumstances.

That was for another day, and being a dutiful daughter, I agreed to dinner. I did enjoy seeing my parents, I really did. Just not today, this week, when the newness of whatever was burgeoning between me, Jordan, and Kade consumed every waking thought.

My parents didn't do anything in half measures, not even the regular family meal. The concept of eating pizza out of a box, or some other takeout meal, wouldn't enter their minds. Instead, I was treated to a lavish five-course degustation complete with complimentary wines and palate cleansers, along with my brother, Damien.

The conversation that followed was either painfully mundane or full of business jargon. My father and Damien spent a good twenty minutes over the main course discussing the impacts of a recent attack on Damien's shipping profit margins. After which, my mother questioned me about my therapy practice and how I was settling into my apartment.

All the while, I fidgeted in my seat, wondering why Jordan and Kade hadn't messaged me. Their job in security had to be dangerous, right?

The exercise in awkwardness was further compounded by my brother's insistence that he take me home afterward.

"So, how are you really settling?" he asked as his skycar made a graceful ascent to join the skyway, where he slipped it into autopilot.

"I really am good," I said.

"Not getting any urges to travel again, are you? Our parents are glad to have you home."

It was as close as he might come to saying he was also glad to have me home.

"No plans to go anywhere," I said, thinking about Kade and Jordan again. I itched to check for a message, even though they'd never messaged me once, save for the official communications about therapy.

"Good," he said. "It's safer for you to be on Chimera."

I turned to face him, wondering what had prompted his

question. As a businessman whose assets stretched over several worlds, he must be far better acquainted with intergalactic conflict than me. He had mentioned the attack on Tolis long before official news broke, and even so, I suspected the media had downplayed the severity. "Is it really so bad?"

"The Empire is suffering," he said. "Poor government control and management has left us weakened. We could be so much more than we are. Yes, it's bad, and it will get a lot worse before it gets better, but it can't get better while we have a corrupt government in place."

"Corrupt? How?" I'd never been one for politics. It simply didn't interest me. As was the mandate, I voted and educated myself enough to make an informed choice, but that was as far as it went.

"How can it be anything but corrupt when only alphas are allowed to join the upper ranks?"

The bitterness in his voice was unmistakable, and left me deeply uneasy.

"Don't accept any positions off-planet, no matter how enticing they sound," he advised. "They are desperate for people like yourself with skills in psychology."

"They?" I thought about that job offer I'd received. Therapists, while useful, rarely attracted such impressive salaries.

"Skilled people of all kinds," he said at length.

"I'm happy here, really. After Kix29, I've had enough excitement for a lifetime. You don't need to worry on that score, and neither do our parents."

"Good," he said, directing the skycar out of the skyway toward my apartment.

Only his words left me unsettled, and as I stood before the window of my decadent apartment, staring out at the city thrumming with life and people, I tried to imagine what it must have been like on Tolis, in the heart of the city as it was decimated by Uncorrupted troops storming through, killing and capturing at whim.

On this troubling note, I went to bed.

Kade

We should have been breaking into Abby's apartment. Instead, we returned to Lucian's club, where Jordan was hell-bent on a showdown with the Gecko.

I tried talking him down.

He was having none of it.

I got it—we'd been in a dangerous situation, and it could have gone badly wrong.

We might have been sitting in a cell.

We might not have gotten the shipment.

The virus might have been in Uncorrupted hands.

We'd pulled through, just.

As we drove into the underground parking garage of Peppermint Moon, Lucian's swanky club, the man in question was also arriving.

"We need to talk," Lucian snarled and stalked off toward his office. There was a smeared bloody handprint down the front of his white shirt, so it was fair to assume he'd also had a busy night.

As the door clicked shut, Lucian turned and did a double take as he noticed Jordan's palpable rage. He looked at me in question.

I didn't have an answer, but my eyes shifted toward the internal office door that had always remained shut and where we had long believed the Gecko holed up.

"You need to calm down," I said to Jordan. I shrugged at

Lucian when Jordan began to wear a path on the carpet, muttering death threats under his breath. "We got the batch," I added, setting the small silver case on the table. "We intercepted the handover in Reaper's Revenge."

Lucian eyeballed Jordan. "What the fuck is his problem, then?"

"I'm going to fucking kill you this time!" Jordan called, thumping the internal door with the side of his fist. "Stop hiding behind a door, asshole!"

I wasn't expecting the door to open because it had never opened once in all the time we'd worked for Lucian. When an alpha stepped out, I didn't know who was stunned more—me, Jordan, or Lucian. He had dark hair, dark pants, scuffed boots, and an orange T-shirt with a lewd, tongue wagging, one-fingered saluting gecko.

The Gecko—the alpha, not the one on the T-shirt—looked a lot like Lucian, only younger.

The seconds stretched, and no one moved or spoke. Then a low, violent growl rattled in his chest, and Jordan charged. *Fuck!* I slammed my palm against his chest, cutting him off, barely.

"It wasn't my fucking fault!" the Gecko said, stalking toward us, which was very fucking stupid. Jordan's rage was giving him the edge, and I thought he was a heartbeat away from clocking me to get to the asshole.

Lucian threw himself into the fray as Jordan and the Gecko hurled insults at one another around us.

"Shut the fuck up, both of you," Lucian roared. "Or I'll shoot you in the nearest non-vital body part until you do!"

I glanced over my shoulder to find Lucian holding a gun to his younger mirror image.

"My head? Really, you're going to shoot me in the fucking

head?" the Gecko said. "Go ahead, that gecko sanctuary could do with some more cash!"

"Gecko sanctuary? What the fuck? Is he crazy?" Jordan demanded, but he wasn't fighting me anymore and sounded as confused as I was.

"Yes," Lucian replied, holstering his gun and throwing a look heavenward. "Jordan, Kade, meet my brother, Rhett."

Silence followed as I processed that. Yeah, the resemblance was strong, except Rhett looked like he had been sleeping in an alley, while Lucian was all sharp suits...and blood.

Jordan heaved a breath, dragged out a nearby chair, and slumped into the seat. "We got our asses handed to us. If Black and Sherwin hadn't been there, no way would we have gotten the shipment. This isn't a fucking game, asshole. You've got some explaining to do."

The Gecko, aka Rhett Banner, did, and none of it was good.

And just like that, all our plans to claim a sweet gamma were put on hold.

Chapter Fifteen

Abby

I didn't see them for a week. A whole week. It was the longest week of my life, and then a new client appointment popped up in my books for Kelvin and Jude, and I wasn't about to refuse.

The day passed in a hazy blur as I convinced myself it both was and was not them.

It was. I nearly threw myself at them when I opened the door and found them sitting in the psychedelic waiting room. Then my breath caught in my throat as I took in all the bruises on their faces and knuckles and worried about the parts I couldn't see.

They hustled me into the room as the first sob broke from my chest and locked the door.

I cried all over Kade. I had no idea what I was crying about, but he picked me up, carried me to the couch, and tucked me in his arms.

Jordan sat opposite, but I didn't like that and told him as much.

"I can't," he said. "If I touch you, you're going to find yourself strapped down in that fucking chair with my hook so deep in your cunt, we'll never be apart. But we can't, not now. We have too much going on, and most of it is dangerous."

I stared at him through tear dampened lashes as I took all this in.

"If we touch you, we're going to mate you...claim you, and we can't do that to you, not now. Better if everyone thinks we're really here for therapy."

"Fuck this up, and I will tear apart every floor in that building until I find the grubby hole where you play at god," Jordan had said back at Kix29. *"Lucian doesn't employ us for our conversational skills. Give me half a reason, and I'll acquaint you with some of them."*

During the stress of the attack, I'd dismissed these comments. With hindsight, I shouldn't have. They were deltas, and as I looked at them, I came to understand that I deserved some answers, that we were all far enough along this path that we understood the parameters of play.

"What do you do?" I asked quietly, subconsciously seeking the comfort of Kade, even as I felt a distance grow. "And don't think about lying to me. I deserve the truth." I wasn't one for making ultimatums, but I thought we could all feel it in the air. My parents had brought me up with a strong sense of self-respect. I wanted them, maybe even needed them, but whatever this was between us, I was going in with my eyes wide open.

"We work for a man called Lucian Banner," Jordan said, "He's a businessman here on Chimera. He owns a number of companies, but you probably know of Peppermint Moon and the fight club Mantis."

"And what do you do for him?" I asked, directing my question at Jordan, because I understood he was the one who called the shots in the duo. "Give me a vague answer like security again, and you can both leave the room."

Kade's hands tightened around my waist, and a tic thumped in Jordan's jaw. My lips gave a telling tremble, but I wasn't backing down.

"We are security. Head of security," Jordan explained. "Lucian is the kind of man who needs a specific kind of security."

I frowned, trying to process that and not liking where my swirling thought pattern was taking me. "He's not only a businessman, is he?"

Jordan shook his head slowly. "No, not a regular businessman, and sometimes, the security work for him can be" —he pinned Kade with a look before redirecting his focus to me— "hands-on."

The tremble in my lips had shifted to the rest of my body.

"Is he a criminal?" I asked softly.

"Fuck's sake," Kade murmured. "She doesn't need—"

"He is," Jordan cut him off. "A powerful one."

I felt the tension spike through Kade, and it lit an echo in me. I tried to get up to create some distance, because this was a lot to take in.

"Uh-uh, sweetheart," Kade said. "Not fucking happening, not until you hear us out. If you want us to fuck off after, we'll fucking go."

Jordan growled at Kade, low and menacing in his chest.

"We'll fucking go," Kade repeated. "But you're going to hear it all first."

"All? What more is there to hear?" Tears streamed down my face. I had missed them so badly, then they turned up covered in bruises, talking about dangerous work, that it was better if people thought they were just here for therapy. Was my mere association with them putting me in danger...putting my family in danger?

Heart thudding wildly, I shoved Kade.

Then another set of hands were on me, big, calming, another purr joining Kade's manic one, and my anger collapsed, leaving me cold, shaky, and confused.

I'd have liked to claim I was only starting to fall for them, but in my heart I'd already fallen deep.

"Have you ever killed someone?"

"Yes."

No hesitation, not even a minuscule pause.

"How many?"

"We don't keep a tally, sweetheart," Kade said, fingers rubbing soothing circles at the back of my neck. "More than are easy to count."

There, they had just admitted they were criminals who killed people at the whim of their boss. I was a therapist who found joy in helping others to live a better life. We were opposites in every conceivable way.

I felt sick.

It didn't matter how I tried to play this out, it would end in tears. Better those tears be done sooner rather than later. It hurt now. It would hurt a thousand times more later on.

"I can't do this. You both need to leave."

"It's not what you think," Kade said, and I could feel his lips against my hair, tearing at my resolve because it felt so damn good. If I could only close my eyes, I could pretend I didn't know.

"Really? How is it not what I think? Do you or do you not work for a criminal boss? Do you or do you not kill for him? It sounds very black and white to me."

"That's all true," Jordan said. "But it's not the whole truth."

"Then tell me the whole truth," I said. I'd never felt so wretched in my life, so torn, so lost. I'd thought I'd found my missing pieces, but instead, I'd found a black hole that wanted to suck out my soul and dignity.

I watched the tic thumping in Jordan's jaw and knew he wouldn't or couldn't tell me, even before he slowly shook his head. Jordan, who was Jude today but had also been James. I'd only been amused at the subterfuge in using a fake name. Now I wondered how fake the name really was, how many personas they took on in their work for a wealthy businessman who was also a criminal.

"You need to tell me or leave."

"We can't," Jordan gritted out. "Don't ask us to leave, because we won't."

"I'm not asking you. I'm telling you, and make no mistake, you really don't have a choice."

They left. I was glad that they did.

I also hated that they did because afterward, I felt more alone than I'd ever done in my life.

Kade

"You should have just told her the truth," I said. "She needed to know. She will need to know sometime. She's going to be our mate, it's not like we can hide it from her."

"Not today, and not in her damn office," Jordan said. "The Gecko said it was clear, but it's far from ideal. We shouldn't have fucking visited her. I let you talk me into that, and look at what happened."

We'd been snarling at one another all evening. An hour of slugging it out in the gym hadn't come close to cooling our tempers. Between Lucian, Black, and Ryker, we had more shit going on than we could comfortably deal with. We could be called away at any moment, not just by Lucian, but by our other boss.

The crazy world of undercover operations had come for us not long after we left the orphanage. The government liked to pick up vulnerable kids like us, with no parent, sibling, or ties, easily trained and manipulated.

No one had ever paid us attention, so when an official came knocking and said they were impressed with our skills in the underground kickboxing circuit, we'd had nothing to lose. The government trained us in secret, so we were off the books, and that was how they wanted to keep us. It was on one of the operations that we'd crossed paths with Lucian. Suddenly, we had two powerful men vying for us.

It suited the government for us to have a job where no one would look too closely if we disappeared from time to time. It suited Lucian to have two highly trained men with connections in the government working for him.

"I've never regretted anything about our jobs," I said. "Until it stopped us claiming Abby."

"It hasn't stopped us, asshole," Jordan said, pacing before our apartment window like a caged beast. He got like this sometimes. Usually, I'd find a way to calm him, but today, I couldn't give a fuck if he went on a rampage. Anything was better than this roiling sickness in my gut.

I needed my fucking hands on her.

"That's it—we're up," Jordan said, suddenly stalking toward the door.

"Up? What do you mean?" I rose from the couch and stalked after him, barely catching up with him as he slammed out the door. "We're on fucking standby for the big boss. Ethan

Black has been kicking over some nasty shit. They might need us at any time."

"And they can call us just as well from her apartment as from here. We're just going to talk to her, be with her, and supposing we have more than five fucking minutes, we can tell her all the things we should have done but couldn't in her office."

"We're breaking into her apartment?" I dragged on my jacket.

"Yep."

I grinned, falling in step beside him as he headed for the elevator bank. "Little gamma probably thinks she's safe in her fancy apartment with Brownwells security."

He chuckled for the first time in days as the elevator arrived with a bong. "Yeah, I forgot to mention Lucian owns that company when we were talking to her earlier. Must have slipped my mind."

He tapped his ear communicator, and I knew he was calling up the Gecko. "You owe us, asshole, and we're calling in a favor."

Chapter Sixteen

Abby

After that tumultuous conversation with Jordan and Kade, I dashed out of the office, claiming that I wasn't feeling well. They were the last appointment of the day, but the efficient office administrator, Cara, still gave me a funny look. Most evenings, I stayed behind for an hour or two to finish any tasks. Tonight, I needed to be home alone to process everything that had been said.

Tears weren't my thing. As a child, I'd quickly understood that my parents had neither the skills nor the ability to cope with them, so I'd kept my emotions to myself. As I found myself alone in the spacious apartment, though, a lifetime of suppressed emotions caught up. There was no joy in weeping. I got on with life no matter what, but I cried a river as I sat on the decadent leather couch with a glass of wine in my hand and watched the skycars zipping past.

The industry of life and people going about their business soothed me as the tears continued to trickle down.

I felt betrayed on every level, but especially by myself. I had decided that they were the right men for me, under-standing early on that they came from a rough beginning so different from mine. What I hadn't expected was for them to be criminals...killers.

"Have you ever killed someone?"

"Yes."

Why had I asked that question?

Because I needed to know the answer. Now, what the hell would I do with the answer?

We were at war. I dealt with men who killed every day of my life, soldiers who fought against the Uncorrupted, but that was different.

Still, my heart refused to believe they were street thugs.

No, not street thugs, but wealthy criminals, if the quality of their clothes was any indication. The life of a hitman, blindly following their boss' command to kill people, must be very lucrative.

"How many?"

"We don't keep a tally, sweetheart."

The dried cuts and fresh bruises on their knuckles and faces were evidence of what they were. Their beautiful bodies doubtless carried more beneath their clothes. The mere thought of the damage and pain made me want to weep twice as hard.

Despite all this, I still wanted to believe this was all a terrible mistake, that somehow, there would be a good explana-tion. Jordan had implied that there was more to say, but he couldn't tell me.

And wasn't that so very cliché.

I thought whatever else he had to say would only make me feel worse. I couldn't live with them in that kind of life. If nothing else, the stress of trying to act normal, knowing they were using their fists and weapons, would kill me.

What about their victims? Did they deserve to die? Or were they like Jordan and Kade—people who had fallen into corruption and violence?

Dead was dead, final. Was killing to protect or survive in a criminal world better or worse than the war? It must be worse.

I understood the nuances, that there were few to be found between one type of killer and another, that everyone was a hero in their own world. Perhaps they thought they did a service, and those who fell by their hand or action were cruel criminals and the world better with them dead.

Their boss, Lucian, was a judge and jury, and Jordan and Kade were his executioners.

The bottom line was that they weren't what they seemed. I'd presumed they were military at first, then private security maybe. Jordan and Kade were neither of those things. They were hired killers. Then there were the other things going on—the mysterious caller, the sudden need to leave, and then the next time I saw them, Jordan's hands had been bruised and busted. A man didn't get that from a sparring session. I wasn't that big a fool.

I was a therapist. I'd dedicated my life to helping people, and I'd dealt with my fair share of military people and all the issues that came with that. At least with a military soldier, I felt like they had a noble purpose, that he or she was defending us from the Uncorrupted.

How could I be attracted to somebody who killed? It went against every principle I had. All this aside, I still wanted them, and I hated myself because of it.

I hadn't been interested in finding a delta until they crashed into my world. Now I did, only a better, more noble version of them.

As I sipped my wine, I played scenarios where they gave up their violent life for me, where they changed and redeemed themselves. I could accept that. I could be with them in such a circumstance and would even relish the prospect of helping them to reform.

I wanted to laugh at my own naïvety.

How could I ever sleep at night or find peace within myself if I chose them?

I couldn't.

Yet I felt like I was being ripped apart in letting them go.

I needed to talk to someone, but who could I trust with such a complex and delicate subject?

Lilly immediately came to mind, and even though I barely knew her, I sensed she could be a confidant. Except she had just escaped capture by the Uncorrupted, and she was with two controllers now. She would have her own problems to deal with.

No, this was my problem. I already knew what I needed to do—walk away.

It had broken me when they left my office at my request. Ridiculous as it was, I'd wanted them to fight for me and persuade me the way deltas were always supposed to do, to take the choice from me, force me, claim me, mate, and breed me, so I'd have no option but to learn to live with all they were.

Claim. It was such an alien word to a gamma, yet what they wanted was every bit as black and white as the claiming alphas and omegas experienced.

That I even entertained such a thought brought a heavy dose of self-disgust.

Oh, how I had fallen in the worst way possible.

Oh, how bitterly disappointed I was that they had respected my request and walked out. I told myself I didn't want them or their unwelcome pursuit, but it was a lie.

I had spent the whole evening lying to myself because I was still breaking apart, and the only thing that would make me whole was the feel of them.

We were both unusual dynamics, and it was understandable that I should suffer this pull, an animalistic instinct to meet and mate with my perfect match. I'd lived all my adult life as a gamma, fancied myself superior to omegas because I didn't like the idea of instincts and scents guiding me. Now here I was, desperately wanting to excuse spectacularly bad relationship choices because I couldn't help myself.

I was disgusted with myself for wanting them.

I was especially disgusted with myself for my subconscious bias toward omegas, for my lack of empathy toward the most oppressed dynamic of them all.

The fall was long and the landing hard, so it was little wonder I was needing some space to process.

Only I had no idea what to do next. The foundations of my world were crumbling.

Whenever and however I pulled myself out of this self-inflicted hole, I wasn't going to be the same.

I put my half empty glass on the low table beside the couch and padded through to my bathroom. Here, I took my glasses off and splashed cold water over my face before patting it dry on the decadently soft towel my mother had bought.

As I put the towel down, the shower called to me. I selected my favorite shampoo and body wash, set aside a clean towel, and stripped out of my clothes before stepping into the hot spray.

The pelting water felt good. I couldn't see or feel my tears while the clean water washed them away. I scrubbed my hair and washed my body, losing myself in the simple task.

Feeling marginally better afterward, I wrapped the big fluffy towel around me and combed out my hair. I couldn't see myself in the mirror without my glasses, just a fuzzy human-shaped blob. My vision wasn't terrible, but it also wasn't great. While at home, I knew my way around, and it didn't matter so much.

I padded through to the bedroom...and screamed.

"Got you," the man dressed all in black said.

My next scream never happened because a big, glove-clad hand clamped over my mouth.

Heart pounding furiously in my chest, I strained against the hold, panic clamoring as his strength and power over me became apparent.

Another blurred shape came into view. God help me, there were two of them.

"Ah, sweetheart," a familiar voice said close to my ear. "You didn't really expect us to walk away now, did you? Don't you know anything about deltas?"

Kade eased his fingers from my mouth, giving me the opportunity to scream if I wanted to, even as useless as that would've been, given the quality of build on this apartment. No one would hear.

Still, it wasn't the pointlessness of the action that stopped me from screaming. No, it was the way the leather encased hand enclosing my throat from behind sent my wayward libido rocketing.

I don't want this, I reminded myself, but my body wasn't listening to reason and my mind was already enticed by the opportunity to embrace plausible denial.

"You were ours from the first day we met," the man before me said—*Jordan*. "But if we had any level of restraint, that went out the window when you let us both inside you, took our hooks so sweetly, and came all over our cocks, screaming and begging us for more."

"Now it's game over as far as your independence is concerned," Kade added as Jordan prowled closer, invading my space, making me shiver, only it wasn't from fear.

No, it was heart pounding lust.

Instinctively, I knew that pleading with them, struggling even, wouldn't budge them from the course. They knew my needs better than I did. I was already pulsing between my thighs, anticipating the pain and pleasure of taking them so deeply.

"H-how did you get in?"

"The door," Jordan said casually. He caught hold of the towel over my breasts and nodded to Kade.

"What? No!" Kade relaxed his hold enough for Jordan to pluck the towel away. It landed with a *whoosh* on the floor beside us.

"You know that criminal we mentioned to you earlier, Lucian Banner?" Jordan said, closing gloved fingers over my breast and giving a gentle squeeze. "Well, he owns many companies, and surprisingly, most of them are legit."

He brushed his thumb lightly over my puckered nipple, bringing a heady clench to my pussy as it stirred all the nerves to life.

I swallowed. Somehow, Kade wearing gloves while he touched me made it a whole other level of hot. With only a lamp on and my glasses still in the bathroom, my vision was limited, but I swear I could see his eyes darken as my nipple responded by peaking to a hard point.

"One of those companies is Brownwells security," Jordan continued. "It was easy enough to call in a favor and override the security on your apartment."

"Oh god." I groaned as he caught the nipple between his thumb and finger and gently squeezed.

"She likes that," Kade said, sliding the hand on my waist down to cup me intimately as Jordan continued to torment my nipple. "Want us to stop, Abby?"

My mouth opened on a gasp as Jordan squeezed harder before rolling my nipple. "Please!"

"Please, what?" Jordan demanded. "Please stop?" He cupped my other breast before clasping the nipple, now squeezing both sides cruelly. "Or please don't stop?"

I wriggled, trying to get away, trying to get more.

Kade began to work his gloved middle finger from side to side, slipping it between my folds, brushing it against my aching clit, and working it closer, more intimately. I could tell by the easy way it moved that I was wet, knew he would be able to tell too.

"She feels nice and wet already," Kade said like he could read my damn thoughts.

"Good," Jordan said, staring at me, doubtless reading all the things I couldn't possibly hide. "Finger her nice and deep. She's going to need to be opened up for what I have in mind—the kind of deep fucking that leaves her sore and aching, the kind she will be feeling for days. Before we leave, our little gamma is going to be in no doubt that she belongs to us. Every time she moves, stands, shifts, or breathes, her body is going to remind her how we took her."

Kade

"Fuck," I murmured as my finger slid into her hot pussy so easily. "She's absolutely drenched." I worked my fingers slowly in and out, cock stone hard from the combination of the hot, squelchy sounds as I fingered her and her shocked little gasps.

I tightened my fingers on her throat as I played with her, drawing my fingertip all the way out to circle her clit before plunging deep again, once, twice, then circling her clit, running my tongue over the shell of her ear, and feeling her shudder as I gently nipped. Finally, we had her all to ourselves, right where we needed her—between us.

I didn't even try to talk Jordan down from the cliff. Instead, I followed him down into hell, but I didn't care. She was ours, now and forever. We should have talked to her and explained that we weren't cold-blooded killers. Even the stuff we did for Lucian wasn't killing for the sake of it. If someone crossed us, sure, we went in hard. Lucian didn't tolerate any bullshit. You played hardball with him, and he would hit back twice as hard.

She was a therapist and cared about people's mental health. It was fair to assume she wanted nothing to do with a couple of trained killers, whatever their cause. Even without our occupation, Abby was way out of our league. She was a rich girl with the kind of parents who bought her a fancy apartment that made our suite above Peppermint Moon look like a dump, and it was far from a dump. We were street rats that had come up through the system. She grew up in luxury.

Were we going to let that stop us? Hell fucking no.

There would be a time for words, but it wasn't now, while instincts rode me, leaving me with a laser focused need to stake a claim.

"You got any lube, Abby?" Jordan asked, cupping her cheek to gain her full attention. "Because we're definitely going to need some."

"I—no!" Abby spluttered, clenching down over my finger, which I'd stilled deep inside her.

"Check her nightstand," I suggested. "I didn't get inside her last time, and I'm desperate to have her ass."

Her pussy had a lock on my finger, so I figured she was on board with that too.

I heard the sound of rummaging.

"God! Please let me go!"

She twitched and strained in my hold. I took the opportunity to work a second finger inside her, which was a squeeze, given I still had my gloves on, and provided a nice distraction to Jordan's search. "No can do, sweetheart."

"Got some," Jordan called, and she froze. "And a nice-sized dildo perfect to work her ass up to your cock."

I slipped my fingers from her and directed her around while she spluttered her indignation. Jordan dropped a pillow in the center of the bed as I propelled her forward. I bit back a smirk because the words of protest coming out of her mouth didn't match the body language as she crawled onto the bed with no more than a gentle swat to the ass.

"Legs open, sweetheart." With my hand locked over the back of her neck, I spanked her ass a little firmer this time, and her thighs popped open. Beside us, I could hear Jordan undressing, and I dragged my eyes from her lush ass to see Jordan's ripped body emerge.

I brushed the hair back from her hot cheeks. "I think Jordan's looking forward to hooking you." Her eyelashes lifted, and her eyes locked on Jordan as he kicked his boots off and shucked down his pants. His cock sprang free, thick and long. "You like the look of that, baby? It's going to be inside you soon, filling you up how you need it."

I trailed my hand down her back, over the sweet swell of her ass, and played in her slick pussy, teasing her with my fingertips as she stared at Jordan. He closed his fist around his cock and worked it along the length. My mouth fucking watered. I wanted him inside her, wanted to taste him on her.

Letting off his dick, he collected the lube and vibrator and put them on the bed beside her so she could get a good look at them.

He nodded his head at me. "Get naked."

Jordan

We were really doing this now and totally committed. I hoped no one needed us anytime soon, because I didn't intend to come up for air until Abby was claimed.

I came down beside her on the bed with the lube and dildo on my mind, only I got distracted by the image of her laid out, her ass popped up on a pillow, her short hair falling over her cheek, and the look in her eyes.

A little hurt, a little confused, but also burning with need.

I couldn't fix the first two, not in a day or night. That would take time, but the last one, yeah, I thought I could deliver enough of that to make her forget everything else.

Her hand was curled beside her face, and I gathered it in mine and brought it to my lips to kiss before redirecting it to my cock. Her lips popped open as her fingers closed around my dick. I pushed into her hand, and she squeezed. Fucking heaven.

The bed jostled as Kade sat his heavy ass on the other side. He leaned over her, closed his fingers over hers, and tightened his grip before slowly jacking up and down. My chest burned with all the emotions I felt in having both their hands on me.

I groaned, Kade smirked, and our little gamma gasped.

"He can take it," Kade said. "He can take anything if your

hands are on him, anyway, anyhow. Kiss her, Jordan. I love watching your mouth on hers."

I did, leaning forward and slanting my mouth over hers, feeling her soften and open, then dipping my tongue inside. The bed dipped, and a shiver went through her at the faint click as Kade opened the lube. I kissed her, distracting her, keeping her occupied, swallowing up all those breathy sounds that told me Kade was working his fingers into her ass, and all the while, she grasped my dick like a lifeline, fondling me erratically and driving me fucking nuts.

"Let's turn her over," Kade said, dragging me from the brink of spilling my load all over her hands.

I dragged my lips from hers, breathing heavily, confused about where I was for a moment before it all came crashing back.

"Over you go, sweetheart," Kade said, putting her on her back with the pillow under her ass.

She moaned, that's when I got a good look at what he was doing. Enrapt, I watched as he worked the pink dildo a small way in and out of her ass, but she threw an arm over her eyes. I swear every drop of blood in my body tried to cram its way into my dick as I saw her ass stretch around the tip.

I nodded, then he gave the dildo over to me and leaned down to tongue her fat little clit that was peeking out and begging for attention. My chest heaved as I worked it deeper into her ass, eyes torn between her flushed cheeks, her stretched asshole, and Kade lapping at her clit.

Dildo deep, I leaned down and tongued her clit, tongue clashing with Kade's, tasting her and him. Feeling the tremble in her and realizing she was close, we both lifted our heads.

"Do you think she'll come like this?" Kade asked. "Switch the vibrator on. I want to get her off already."

Abby

I was on my back, my trusty vibrator being used in ways I'd never intended as Jordan worked it in and out of my ass. All the while, Kade performed voodoo on my clit with his tongue.

I was already floating on the cusp when the sudden buzz and the instant vibration in my ass sent me spinning. I arched up as pleasure shot from my clit all the way to my ass, then those tight, resistant muscles began to contract in dark, heavenly waves. God, it felt so raw, earthy, and fluttery, deeper and more intense than anything I'd experienced before.

I was still gasping and tingling when the buzzing abruptly stopped and the vibrator slipped out, but I didn't have time to process the sudden jostling as Jordan loomed over me, lined up, and slammed into me, rough, fast, and dominant.

He just held there, letting me get used to the stretch as Kade redirected his attention to my breast, sucking gently as if to soothe Jordan's savage penetration.

His hand cupped my cheek, and I blinked up at him, startled by how emotional I suddenly felt, wishing I could see him better but unwilling to stop proceedings for my glasses, even supposing they might accommodate such a request.

My ass throbbed and tingled from the climax, feeling strongly bereft without the attention, and my hips pushed up because I suddenly wanted and needed more.

"She's ready," Jordan said, his voice all gravelly with his lust.

"Agreed," Kade said.

Then we were rolling. Jordan ended up on his back and me on top, with him still buried inside me. The position heightened the stretch.

Regrets loomed on my periphery, but I paid them no heed. I couldn't exist without them, turning desolate at the mere thought of letting my men go. Heat blanketed my back as Kade settled behind me, his hands gentle as they found my hips. One skimmed downward to rest fingertips over my swollen clit. The other moved to cup the back of my head, angling it so he could slant his lips over mine. I opened, and our tongues tangled, heat rising. The faint shake of Jordan's hands as they cupped my breasts told me this was just as serious for him, just as Kade's hot, sweet kiss told me the same.

Deep inside, a thick cock flexed, and my pussy squeezed in delight.

They took their time, hands moving over my body, lips giving gentle nips, awakening the nerves along the surface of my skin to their touch, and all the while, I was filled, aware of them and of what was to come.

Soft begging words only distantly registered as mine, while the gentle, coaxing kiss from Jordan encouraged me to lean forward—a position that allowed Kade room to slide the tip of his cock around the sensitive rosebud of my ass.

It felt good, even that light touch. My impatience rose as Kade withdrew and applied more lube.

I was too far gone to worry, wanted the completion, to have them both inside me, to bind them to me, even as they sought to do the same. They had prepared me well, and there was only the slightest hitch in my breath as the very tip of Kade's cock breached me.

Kade's lips were at my throat as he whispered, "Good girl, relax for me," before more tender kisses and the intense pressure as he sank slowly inside me, aided by copious lube.

Jordan stole my gasp as the stretch registered concern, more and more cock filling me, until Jordan eased out, and Kade sank fully in.

Everything throbbed, giving me a deep, achingly wondrous sensation of being darkly full.

"You good, sweetheart?" Kade asked, the earlier brutality gone, and in its place was a concerned lover, trying to ensure the experience was good.

"Yes," I gasped out, squeezing over him. "God, please move."

"Whatever the lady wants," Kade said gruffly, and oh, I felt the most sublime pleasure ripple through me as he pulled out and Jordan surged in.

Why had I ever feared this?

What was more perfect than the sensation of being filled first one way and then the other, fluttering nerves and switching my focus, sending me rising and heat coursing through me?

"I'm going to come."

"Come then," Jordan said, teeth nipping at my throat.

Time lost meaning as I rose toward that glorious high and pitched straight over the rhythmic waves into bliss, and a laugh bubbled up, which turned into a gasp as Jordan thrust up just a little rougher.

"Yes!" I hissed my encouragement, nails finding flesh and sinking in, a growl of approval encouraged me to sink them deeper.

Their strokes never stopped over intimate places that became over sensitized, making me twitch and whine.

"Come again," Kade encouraged, fingers sliding back and forth over my clit. "Come for us, sweetheart."

I had no choice but to comply, hands, lips, and hard cocks driving me into white-hot pleasure. I groaned and clenched over hot flesh, eyes closed because even the soft light of my lamp was too bright.

"Come again," Jordan rumbled, his teeth raking over my

nipple, fingers biting into my hips to hold me still as he slammed into me from below.

I shook my head, but my body was not mine anymore. It was theirs.

I came.

Again and again.

It was only later, when the urgency did not abate and my once gentle lovers began to pound into me together, that I understood the magnitude of the storm.

More.

We were all sweaty skin, teeth, and nails, the slick passage of hot thrusting flesh consuming me.

The taste of blood on my tongue was *satisfying*.

The relentless pounding demanded I give *more*, receive *more*.

I knew there would be bruises, but I didn't care.

I needed *more*.

I needed to be one.

Pain came but was smothered instantly by shuddering, breathtaking rapture that took me to the highest heights then tossed me to the ground.

Love.

Throbbing, pounding blood rushed through the veins of our hot, sweaty bodies, our chests heaving as lungs strove to get more air, but the pleasure never stopped.

I was so full—blissfully full.

Perfect.

Ours.

The voices were inside me, just like their hot, perfect cocks, jetting cum into me as they staked their claim.

Chapter Seventeen

Abby

I came to awareness in increments, finding myself plastered against a wall of male flesh. Inside was an alien itch, a presence—no, two presences.

We had bonded.

Bonded for life.

I rose to a sitting position, grasping my chest, unable to breathe through the constriction in my throat.

"Abby, sweetheart?" Kade said, fingers smoothing through my hair. "Just breathe, baby. We've got you."

Only I didn't want to be *got*. What the hell had I done?

Abby!

The second presence manifested in the arrival of a dripping wet Jordan at the bedroom door, and just like that, from merely staring at him, the way he planted his hands on his hips, his thick cock flexing as my eyes lowered toward it.

When I could tear my gaze away from that arresting sight, I found his nostrils flared and his eyes boring into me, and I

169

could breathe, but only if I was breathing for him. Kade might be a wall of muscle and handsome, but he didn't have the same dominant presence as Jordan, which sent little sparks skittering across my skin.

"I don't tolerate any nonsense, Abby," he said.

Nonsense?

"You need to back off," Kade said, voice soft and dangerously low. "She's newly bonded. It's new for all of us."

Jordan's eyes twitched, like he was considering thumping Kade.

"Fine, she was having a panic attack," Kade said, tone full of snark. "Your asshole ways stopped it. What do you want, a fucking medal?"

Jordan's lips tugged up before he redirected his attention to me.

I sensed their preexisting relationship during that exchange and felt myself as something new inserted between them. They had a history together that stretched over ten years, the latter part of it sexual in nature.

I swallowed, aware of Jordan's cock twitching vigorously and refusing to look or acknowledge it. We really needed to talk, since we had just committed to each other for forever, yet my entire focus shifted to the way my body ached.

"The kind of deep fucking that leaves her sore and aching," Jordan had said when they first broke into my apartment. *"The kind she will be feeling for days. Every time she moves, stands, shifts, or breathes, her body is going to remind her how we took her."*

And I was, gloriously so. My pussy, ass, and belly clenched in anticipation for one or both of them being inside me again.

How I had fallen, and how addicted I had already become.

My cheeks flushed, and the air electrified as I became

aware of them on the minutest level, of their breathing, of their arousal.

"I don't think I can handle it in my..." I trailed off. What was wrong with me? It was like I'd forgotten how to assert myself. "Neither of you are putting anything in my ass."

That I ached inside and out didn't stop me from wanting them. I was about to be fucked. We were yet new to one another, and the passion burned brightly. Filthy and a little crusty in places, I should definitely not be aroused, unless they were about to take me for the shower Jordan had just enjoyed.

Jordan stalked toward me, his grin taking on a decidedly wolfish gleam. "If your ass is off the table, that's okay. We have plenty of other options." As he reached the bottom of the bed, his eyes shifted fleetingly to Kade.

Were they communicating in the same way? Their words formed in my mind that I knew to be theirs, leaving a tone, a *taste*, that indicated who had spoken. I got the distinct impression that they could also talk without me, by choice. Had they always had this ability, or was it new to our bonding?

My chest rose and fell unsteadily, my pussy emitting a deep ache as sore muscles clenched.

"Clean her up," Jordan said, eyes still on me, although it was Kade he was talking to. I expected Kade to take me to the bathroom, but he didn't. Instead, he tumbled me onto my back, spread my thighs wide, and buried his face between them.

I gasped, my fingers closing tightly over his hair, because damn, the sensation of his tongue lapping over the soreness was heaven. Kade groaned, licking and lapping like he was in heaven too.

"Please, I need to clean up," I protested, making a concerted effort to rediscover a sense of decorum.

"Exactly," Jordan said. "Kade is cleaning you all up."

My breath was already turning into a pant, sensitivity and

pleasure blooming. The image of Kade between my thighs, his big hands holding me open, my whole body on display, only heated me further, especially when my gaze lifted to see Jordan's interest.

Jordan approached, hand sliding over Kade's back from hip to nape in a dominant move I felt all the way to my core. My stomach performed a slow tumble as his fingers wrapped around Kade's throat to hold him against me. His mastery over both of us was evidenced in that move. If I ever had any doubts as to who dominated this exchange, they were rendered null and void. Lust pummeled me through the bond, both mine and theirs.

They were so close, hips almost touching, Jordan's cock leaking a trail of clear stickiness all the way to Kade's ass.

Eyes locked on mine, Jordan could see my interest, even were it not for the bond. "Do you want me to fuck him?"

Kade growled against my pussy in the most arresting way. I'd imagined them together, wondered how it would work, two such powerful and dominant men being intimate with one another, being vulnerable. Seeing them touch lightly brought a sharp, achy clench of approval.

I nodded slowly.

"This is gonna get rough," Jordan said, skimming both hands over Kade's ass, "but you can take it. Show our mate how much you enjoy a deep reaming from my cock, how much you love it."

Kade's hands tightened on my thigh, biting into the flesh as he lapped up my swollen clit, sending me higher, making me twitch, desperate to come but wanting to hold it just a little longer, because it felt so unbearably good.

Jordan's gaze lowered as he took his cock in hand, palm against Kade's ass, pulling him open. His tongue darted over his lips in concentration, and he gave a low rumble as he focused and pressed forward.

Kade's head popped off me, glaring over his shoulder, then snarled at the male behind him, "Get on with it."

Jordan only smirked as he took Kade's hips and slammed in. The raw pain and pleasure were evidenced in the way his face contorted, teeth gritted.

"Fuck, you feel good." Jordan grunted. "Keep your hands off your cock. You'll come when I say, when Abby's gotten off."

Kade nipped at my inner thigh before planting his face in my pussy, eating me out, tongue delving deep before flicking all over my clit.

Jordan began to pound into Kade, the tight muscles of his abdomen, shoulder, and chest straining and flexing, while I, wanting to watch, fought the pull to close my eyes.

Mouth hanging slack, I gave into the pull, the vision of them moving against one another, brutally perfect.

I came—I had no choice. The spasms ripped through me, demanding release. Only Kade didn't stop, and neither did Jordan, so barely had I landed then I was soaring again.

They came with me that time, with grunts of pleasure, ragged breaths, and the white-hot bliss that was theirs and mine.

Afterward, we collapsed, sweaty, filthy, and not even caring.

Jordan moved first, staggering up, and the sounds of a shower running followed.

I dozed, sore but content, not ready to open my eyes and break the spell.

The decision was taken from me when Jordan ordered Kade to bathe me. Like the dutiful second he was, Kade carried me through to a prepared bath. He let me soak in the bubbles as he showered before returning and washing me with the care that belied he was a killer, with bruises still on his knuckles and faint bruising along his jaw.

Squeaky clean, he helped me to dry before carrying me back to the freshly made bed. I presumed Jordan must have made it before ordering some food. I was ravenous and giddy with excitement at the thought of food.

"You okay?" Kade asked, brushing damp hair from my forehead.

I nodded, conscious of this new intimacy, which made no sense given all the things we had done. The center of my chest itched, and a strange tugging sensation like a thread was buried there.

"We wondered how you would be, seeing us together." He grinned. "Knowing you were watching him fuck me was insanely fucking hot."

"You're so dominant, I couldn't imagine how you might be together."

"I'm not dominant."

My chin lifted, and I studied him. "But you're... You seem very dominant with me."

He smirked. "I like to please people. I get off on it."

My face flushed. "I'm not sure I'm comfortable with that... with you doing something just to please Jordan or me."

"Why not?" Kade asked, frowning now.

"Because I—" I was a therapist, for goodness' sake, who had studied human behavior as it pertained to all kinds of dynamics and non-dynamics. I understood that some people liked to please others, but for a start, Kade had no issue asserting himself, which meant this was only sexual in nature. Was this healthy or not? Was his dominant act even disingenuous? My brain turned a little foggy, and I floundered for an answer because now I was thinking about the rough fucking and how their pleasure had bombarded me.

"I feel uncomfortable with you faking something," I said at length. "Like the experience isn't equal if I take more and you give more. I want you to be yourself and to act however feels right for you. If that is less dominant, then I will love it too, because it is you."

"You're not listening, sweetheart," he said. "Telling me not to please you is confusing and makes me feel lost. I don't like feeling lost." He shook his head. "I fucking hate that feeling." Rolling above me, he pinned my hands above my head and dropped a fraction of his considerable weight on me to squish me into the bed.

My heart rate jacked up, and my pussy spasmed tightly. His hot gaze only revved my wayward libido further.

"I like pleasing you." His eyes roamed over my face like he was cataloging every tell. "I like that little breathy catch when I do something that arouses you. It makes me hard as fuck. How are you taking advantage of me? It feels right to please you. You and Jordan are the center of my world."

He slid his hard cock against me, catching my clit and making me groan.

"There, right there," he said. "Your face, the way it scrunches up with pleasure, and that sound you make, like it's being torn from deep inside, all raw and honest. I fucking crave that sound. I'd do fucking anything for more of that sound... Now Jordan *is* dominant to the core. He also wants to please you but in a very different way—in ways you don't think you can handle but definitely need."

The power I felt over Kade—over Jordan too—was both overwhelming and humbling. This huge male pinning me to the bed, sliding his erection into my most intimate place with calculation, wanted only to please me. If he was rough with me, it was because his attentive focus told him it was what I needed. It dawned on me that even when he terrified me, I had only ever been wildly aroused. Not once had I been unwilling. It rocked me to realize how deeply Kade was attuned to me, how they both were, and how safe I was with them, emotionally and physically.

How did someone so incredible come out of all the ugly their lives had done to them? I wanted to hate what had happened, the binding, but I couldn't. As I'd decided not so long ago, I would find a way to live with them. I caught myself on the brink of hoping they might change for me. No, I wouldn't go into this with delusions.

"Don't be sad, Abby," he said, tone soft as he cupped my cheek.

My heart broke a little at the rawness of his words.

For better or worse, I was bound to them.

Chapter Eighteen

Abby

We didn't make it more than two minutes into enjoying the delicious takeout when a call came.

I didn't need to ask. Jordan's body language as he paced before the window, the way Kade had frozen, watching him like I did, said whatever was coming would not be to my liking.

"We need to go," Jordan said, and that fast, the glow disappeared. "I'm sorry." He swiped a hand through his hair, sounding as exasperated as I felt.

"Go where?" I asked. It was too early to make demands, or perhaps it was just right.

"Lilly has been taken," he said.

Cold settled in the pit of my stomach. "Lilly? As in Dr. Lillian Brach?"

He nodded. Kade didn't even question him. He just stalked through to the bedroom, where I could hear him dressing.

"Can I help?" I didn't have a clue what I might be able to do that was useful, but I was in shock and not thinking at my best.

"No, Abby," Jordan said. He cupped my cheeks and searched my eyes before lowering his lips to mine.

I could taste the danger in the kiss, the desperation in him not to leave, yet he had to.

Kade returned, dressed and looking strangely lost. "Sorry," he said. Then he was kissing me, and I was clinging, unable to let go, forcing him to pull my fingers away. The pain of that disconnect felt like the slow rot of death in the center of my chest.

"We need you to keep safe for us," Jordan said. "We'll be back as soon as we can, and then we'll talk."

They left. I watched the door close and could not process what any of this meant.

I wept for the second time in my adult life.

It was only later, as I stared at the ceiling in my bedroom, convincing myself their scent was around me, even if I couldn't tell, that I realized something was off.

Why were two men, criminal hit men by all accounts, helping in such a delicate operation?

My brows pinched together.

Had they lied?

No, I was confident that they had not.

Unfortunately, I didn't have any answer to this puzzle, at least none that made any sense.

A fluttery sensation settled in my chest.

If I wanted answers, I would have to wait until they returned.

Chapter Nineteen

They called themselves the Uncorrupted because the virus didn't touch them.

For better or worse, the virus had been released and genetic mutation had occurred, resulting in the thirteen dynamics who now made up a large portion of the population.

The Uncorrupted called it a cleansing. I called it genocide.

~ Doctor Lillian Brach

Abby

It had been three weeks since Jordan and Kade exited my apartment—three long and painful weeks, where I tried to carry on as normal.

Inside, I was crumbling and barely holding it together, living under a cloud of worry about my mates and Lilly.

Mates. Yes, I'd had plenty of time to come to terms with my new status and what it meant. We never did get that conversation, but in some ways, being without them helped for me to come to terms with my changed life, time to understand that there would be some pain ahead as we navigated our relationship. I hadn't told my parents yet. I wasn't ready to broach the subject so new and as yet not fully realized.

So I carried on, knowing that change was coming and that nothing I did could prepare me for their return.

It was a bright, sunny morning as I made my way to the prestigious offices of Varro & Bright. I'd sent them a message saying their job offer wasn't for me before Jordan and Kade left. They had expressed surprise, which was to be expected, given the offer was double my current rate, plus numerous other benefits, and besides that, it sounded like fascinating work. Then a few days ago, there came an additional offer for me to choose from their other locations since Ridious had not been to my liking. I'd never visited Ridious, but I'd heard it was a cosmopolitan place with dynamics of every kind. I wasn't averse to it per se, but somewhere between my conversation with Ryker where I'd hinted at leaving, my brother's warning, and Jordan and Kade breaking into my apartment, I'd already dismissed off-world living. Now that I was mated, any such possibility was well and truly gone.

After I refused their second job offer, they had asked me if I would mind being interviewed for their research, as one of the doctors had some questions for me based on my work for the military. I didn't, since knowledge sharing was part of any industry, and therapists and physiologists often discussed learnings and the latest research. I was always happy to oblige and hadn't hesitated to accept the request. Further, I'd been keen to arrange the meeting sooner rather than later.

Exiting the transport hub, I took the final short walk to the prestigious building where Varro & Bright had offices. A fast elevator whisked me fifty floors up, where I entered a plush reception area with a glass door and a fancy silver logo.

The first thing I noticed was that it was quiet, unnaturally so, with a single lady sitting in the reception who, unusually, was a non-dynamic. I wasn't a snob about a person's dynamic status, but my opinion that they rarely assumed such positions was based on cold hard facts. They were at the bottom of the dynamic food chain for many and varied reasons, the most notable being that they simply lacked intelligence or skills for more nuanced work. It wasn't a fair world. The copper virus wasn't culpable for this. It had merely exaggerated what was already there. Many non-dynamics were hardworking citizens who lived and contributed within their means, but many were also criminals by opportunity or simply because they were so inclined. Not that non-dynamics had the monopoly on poor social behavior, because every caste, except perhaps omega or mu, were capable of committing crimes. Non-dynamics were more often involved with lone crimes, such as thievery, assaults, and even murders. They were not criminal masterminds, although many fell down the corrupt path because the gangs picked them up as easy prey for their cause. So while the majority were hardworking members of the labor force, they rarely rose to office work, and certainly not in prestigious companies like this.

Maybe I was mistaken and she was simply a less familiar dynamic to me? No, I'd always had a sixth sense about such things.

"How can I help you?" she asked politely.

"Abby Winters," I said. "I have an appointment with Dr. Rook."

She smiled. "Of course. I'll show you straight through."

She rose, rounded the desk, and escorted me along a corridor before showing me into a room empty save for a large mirror on one wall and a desk with a chair on either side. There were no windows, and the ambiance left me feeling strangely trapped.

"Please take a seat," she said. "Dr Rook will be along shortly."

"Thank you," I said, drumming up a smile as I took the nearest seat. I'd seen my share of multipurpose offices and rooms, but this one was particularly soulless.

The door shut behind her with a heavy clunk.

My eyes went to the mirror, and I shuddered, trying to shake off the notion of being watched. It was odd to find a mirror when more often, it was an interactive whiteboard or screen.

No mind, Dr. Rook would be along presently, and once the interview was done, I would be back home, waiting for a certain two men to return.

I smiled, despite my worries, thinking about that last conversation with Kade. I should get some therapy for myself, like Lillian Brach had suggested. Then there was the mystery around them being called up to help with Lilly's return. I didn't want to get my hopes up or build up scenarios in my mind, only to have them crushed.

One step at a time, and it would all work out.

The door opening stirred me from my musing, and a man entered. "Dr Rook, I'm pleased to meet you," I said.

He didn't say anything, just strode straight over to take the seat opposite me.

Was it Dr. Rook? The man before me was a theta, I was sure of it, and although it should have comforted me, given I was well acquainted with the caste, it did not.

The skittering sensation that had manifested on entering the reception returned in full force as he unfolded a slim tablet and placed it on the table between us.

"Abby Winters," he said. "Gamma, currently working as a therapist."

"Yes, that's me." I smiled, although it felt fake on my lips. "Are you Dr. Rook?" I glanced over my shoulder at the door, half expecting it to open and the real Dr. Rook to enter.

"I am," he said. "I'm very impressed with your resumé." He indicated the tablet. "You have an exemplary reputation for offering therapy to dynamics of every kind, but in particular, alphas."

"Yes," I said, a little breathless and definitely stressed. "I work with quite a few betas too—"

"We're not interested in the betas," he said, cutting me off.

Okay, that had been abrupt, borderline rude, but plenty of people lacked social skills, and thetas were renowned for brusque ways.

"Did you know about the government's viral program to increase dynamic yields?"

"Yes, I did. I met Lillian Brach briefly when I was on Tolis." I didn't mention that she was missing and wondered how many people actually knew. It hadn't been on the news, and I'd been looking.

"Do you think you will see her again?" he asked, tapping away on his tablet.

What a strange question. Was this supposed to be a theta *getting to know you* conversation? If it was, it was sorely lacking.

My eyes lowered to his tablet, although I couldn't see his writing from here.

"I don't suppose I will, unless she requested it for some reason. Why do you ask?"

"We're keen to interview Dr. Brach," he said. "But let's focus on you today, Abby, if I may call you Abby."

"Of course," I said. My eyebrows pinched together that he

didn't offer me a similar courtesy of his first name. I was a doctor like him, and he didn't need to stand on ceremony.

"We also have an alpha program."

"You do?" My frown deepened. "I didn't realize the private sector was involved in such things."

"Yes," he said, "The program has been running for several years, but we are having some...issues."

"I'm not sure how much help I can provide in an hour, but I'm happy to share anything I can."

"This isn't only an hour."

"Oh, were you planning more interviews? Nobody mentioned that before. My client books are very busy at the moment." I really didn't want to have another interview. This one was already weird enough, and we were only five minutes in.

"I believe you are laboring under a misunderstanding here, Abby," he said, fingers busy on the keyboard again. "You're far too valuable for us to allow you to leave. The issues with the program are substantial. The alphas are prone to the darker traits not usually associated with their kind, at least not the Empire's alphas. Aggression is natural among the caste, but not the ruthlessness we are seeing. Perhaps it's environmental. One doesn't survive in the Uncorrupted ranks easily, and infighting is part of the norm—dog, eat dog, I'm sure you've heard. Still, we'd like the alphas more...manageable if they're to meet our needs."

My mouth hung open as words tried to form and failed. "The Uncorrupted," I finally managed to squeeze past the tightness in my throat.

He nodded. "Exactly—the Uncorrupted." He smiled. "Varro & Bright, and a number of similar companies, are merely a front and facilitate us finding dynamics useful to the cause."

"You're not a theta," I said slowly, lips trembling as this realization settled in. He was intelligent, had everything about the caste except that final part. He was Uncorrupted and had never been subjected to the virus. Were he exposed to it now, I had every reason to expect he would manifest. The woman in the reception was also a non-dynamic but perhaps might have manifested as a beta.

Only they were pure, original humans, not a non-dynamic because the virus had passed them by, but because they had left the Empire long ago and had never chosen to be exposed.

Hearing the distinct sound of a heavy lock bolting into place, my head snapped around. My body refused to accept what my mind was screaming—I was trapped, and I had just unwittingly become a victim of the Uncorrupted's dynamic trafficking. Suddenly, my brother's warning held a deeper meaning. Did he know about this?

I stumbled from my chair, taking the few steps needed to pound uselessly on the door.

No one came.

Dr. Rook didn't offer a response, and when I turned back, shaking with betrayal and fear, he was observing me casually from his chair. "How can you do this to innocent people?"

He sneered suddenly in his first real show of emotion. "Innocent? Have you ever seen an Uncorrupted world after an attack?"

My chest heaved at the vitriol in his tone. No, I hadn't. There were always two sides to a war. I'd never thought about it much, for it had never touched my life beyond reports on the news.

My wide eyes darted toward the mirror I now suspected to be one-way glass.

"You will make a wonderful addition," he said.

My lips trembled. "If you take me, I'll only die, and that wouldn't be very useful for your cause."

"Dramatic of you, Dr. Winters," he said, smiling faintly. "You're referring to your recent bonding with the delta males."

My mouth opened and closed. "How could you..." But of course he knew. He was working for the Uncorrupted and had targeted me. No one did that without thorough groundwork.

"If you are thinking they might save you. I dare say they will try. In fact, we are counting on them doing exactly that."

"They won't." I said, only it lacked confidence. Jordan and Kade would die trying to free me. "And even if they did, they won't succeed. They're just security managers. Why would you even want them to?" If I felt cold terror for myself, it was nothing to the horror that assailed me at thinking of Kade and Jordan being hurt, possibly killed, trying to save me.

"You're referring to their work for Lucian Banner? The business mogul is just a front. They work for the government and have done so long before Banner came along. We've had our eye on them for a while. Now we have you, it's a given they will come, then we'll have all of you as a nice package deal. Fear for you will keep them in line, and fear for them will keep you similarly compliant." He shrugged casually as if my dreadful fate were of little consequence to him...and it really was. "Sorry, this is necessary. I promise you, it won't hurt."

Drawing a mask from his pocket, he slipped it over his nose and mouth. My protest died on my lips, and a second later, blackness came for me.

He'd said it wouldn't hurt. Later, when I woke up, I realized he had lied.

Chapter Twenty

Jordan

I t had been three long weeks since we'd seen Abby, and I was ready to climb the walls of the battered—should have been scrapped—ship that Ethan and Ryker had mysteriously commandeered for the rescue of Lillian Brach.

The omega was back safely under the care of her two mates, and none of them had come up for air the entire journey back to Chimera, not that I could blame them. Had Abby been here, I'd have been balls deep, getting better acquainted with our mate.

Except she wasn't here, she was back on Chimera, and as the docking notification came through, the restlessness that sometimes consumed me came back full bore.

Kade and I hadn't fucked once since we'd left, not even in the quieter, stress free downtime during the return. We'd both agreed that it didn't feel right. We were no longer a couple. We had a mate, one that tied us together in a different way, one we needed to respect. It would take frequent conversations and time to find rules that worked for all of us.

I didn't feel jealous of her myself. The thought of Kade fucking her while I wasn't there only made me hungry. Kade and I didn't always work together, and circumstances often led to one of us being on one job while the other was elsewhere, although we preferred to have each other's back. Still, I could imagine returning home and Kade telling me all about what he'd done with her while I was gone, and our sweet little mate getting all hot and embarrassed and yeah, she'd definitely be turned on.

That was for later. First, we needed to reconnect as a thruple and learn about each other.

Kade and I left our quarters and headed out to the galley. Once we docked at the space station, we'd be taking a shuttle down to the planet side port.

Ryker was already standing by the airlock, tapping manically on a piece of piping hanging off the wall. Ethan was sitting to his right with Lilly in his arms.

I did a double take at seeing all the bites and scratches over Ryker's arms and throat. It looked like an animal had been at him. *Lucky bastard.*

He nodded at us and grinned. "So what's the deal with you and the little gamma?"

"None of your fucking business," I snarled. I wasn't ready to go public with our mating yet, so his nosy assed comment grated on my already thin nerves.

"You know she's leaving, right?"

"The fuck are you talking about?" Kade asked before I could demand the same.

Ryker's smile dropped, and he held up both hands. "Seriously, don't shoot the fucking messenger. If you guys don't talk, it's not my fault."

"She's not leaving," I said because she wasn't. Except we barely knew her and had broken into her apartment and claimed her without so much as a word of discussion, not that it would have mattered.

Ryker's face did that little scrunching thing that said we were both idiots and he really didn't want to get involved, which was too fucking bad now he'd opened his mouth.

I had him by the throat against the galley wall a beat later. Given it was only partially paneled and crap of every kind was sticking out, I doubted he was faking the wince.

"Don't break anything vital," Ethan called. "Lilly really likes him."

I growled. "Explain yourself."

"She said she was leaving, had a job on a remote space station. I asked her if she would still do my therapy remotely. She said she would try to work something out."

I let him go.

"Damn," Kade muttered. "I don't think that he's making that up just to piss you off."

An announcement came through from the space station clearance team, notifying us to disembark and bringing an end to the conversation.

Ryker, wisely, kept his mouth shut. I was sinking into a dark mood, and only one thing would pull me back from it—seeing our mate again, having her explain that this was all a misunderstanding and that Ryker was mistaken.

Only I knew Ryker wasn't mistaken. We'd gotten to know the alpha over the weeks since we'd met, working with him to follow up on leads for the omega drug and later to rescue Lilly. He was a first-class prick, but he wouldn't lie about this.

I was pissed that she was leaving.

I was also fucking terrified that she was leaving.

"You don't think she'll be gone yet, do you?" Kade asked. He sounded lost, and I fucking hated it. It gutted me to hear the tremble in his voice, feeling his pain echo my own. "You don't think we drove her away, do you?"

Yeah, that fear gutted me even deeper.

The Empire was never a safe place ever, but it was worse at the moment. The Uncorrupted were spreading, and even Chimera wasn't safe. They were getting bolder, seeking the rarer dynamics, particularly female omegas. A gamma was far too close to that for comfort.

It was a tense wait while we docked and then took the shuttle planet side. As soon as we got a signal, we got a message from Rhett, Lucian's brother, formerly known as the Gecko.

"Need you in Lucian's basement office, asap."

He was still a fucking gecko lover, but we'd come to a level of understanding whereby I could see him in person without wanting to beat his head through the nearest wall. I still thought about it, but sue me, the guy was still a prize prick who liked to bait me with a reckless disregard for his health.

"We have personal stuff that takes priority," I said. It was the first and only time I'd ever said this.

A long silence followed.

"We need to talk. It's a priority and personal—not for me, but for you—and not something we can discuss over a communicator."

The world was moving fast and slow. I didn't remember anything of the journey to Peppermint Moon, nor how we got to the basement office, where we found Lucien pacing, drawing heavily on a cigar with enough enthusiasm that the air conditioning struggled to keep pace, and sweet tobacco scent perfumed the air.

"Do you know why Abby would go to the Varro & Bright office early yesterday?" Rhett asked. He was wearing the scruffy orange gecko T-shirt again, jeans, no shoes, and messy hair that said he hadn't slept in a week.

I frowned. Lucian would usually be pumping me for details on the op with Black and Sherwin. The lack of questions and his pacing freaked me out on a whole other level.

"Never heard of them," Kade said.

"They advertise jobs from time to time, the kind you need to entice high-flying dynamics—good pay, lots of benefits. Abby entered their offices yesterday, but she never came back out."

The job? The fucking job? I frowned. "What do you mean she never came back out? Another entrance?"

"You got friends in high places," Lucian said. "Might need to call on them. Varro & Bright are a front. I put people on the building as soon as Rhett raised a flag, but several hours had already gone by. We've got nothing, and when I say nothing, I mean I've shaken down every street rat and corrupt fucker I could lay my hands on. They all had one message—be careful what questions you ask about Varro & Bright."

Before I could say more, my communicator bleeped with a priority incoming message.

Chapter Twenty-One

Abby

Dark was how my world felt since I met with Dr. Rook.

Dark was the reality of my world when I woke up in a small square room alone.

The only source of illumination was a dull amber emergency light over the sealed metal door. My knees, shoulder, and wrist ached from the fall after they gassed me.

Such physical pain took a backseat to the sharp hurt in my heart. I put my head in my hands, and I cried for only the third time in my adult life.

I told myself I couldn't have known how this would play out, but self-reproach still beat at me from every direction. I'd been naïve in some respects, yet what other way was there to go through life? Suspecting everyone of everything?

I'd never felt so wretched.

Here I was now, a trap for the two men I loved—two men who were nothing like they'd seemed. The moment Dr. Rook mentioned them working for the government, everything clicked into place, especially the way they'd been called to help with the rescue of Lilly Brach, a high profile dynamic whose father was on the ruling council.

Jordan had said we needed to talk, but time had gotten away from us and they'd left urgently. Were they still searching for Lilly? Was she safe? Was she a prisoner, like me?

I wished they'd told me from the start, wished I'd had the opportunity to know the real them, to not go through the conflict of believing them nothing more than hired hitmen for a wealthy criminal.

They were still that, and the government was aware, perhaps even directing them so they could watch Lucian Banner as part of an undercover operation.

No, that didn't ring true. The way they had spoken about their boss was colored with respect.

None of this mattered. Soon, they would come for me, or try to, and then they would be trapped, too. I'd just unwittingly put two highly skilled killers in the hands of the Uncorrupted, and this besides whatever knowledge they could scrape from me.

Death would have been kinder, yet were it offered to me, I'd still reject it. I'd reject anything for a scrap of time with them, to know that they were still alive.

Misery would be done to all of us.

I wanted to blame myself, yet there was no blame in the cage of the Uncorrupted.

"Have you ever seen an Uncorrupted world after an attack?"

He wasn't a theta, not really, but the coldness in his words led me to understand them for truth.

No one liked to dwell on the ugly side of war, filled with death and killing, not all of it noble. You couldn't kill people without destroying a part of yourself. There were two sides to every conflict, and pain and suffering for both.

No person needed to watch sons or daughters die.

Omegas were naturally altruistic, not having a killer bone in their body, yet the government still deployed them in war, using them as weapons, tracking devices, and healers so that the soldiers could pick themselves up and fight some more.

Despite learning much after the non-disclosure agreement I'd signed, I still hadn't fully understood what it meant. Now and here, on the other side, confronted by my own part, the fog was lifting and bitter enlightenment was mine.

The light above the door switched to green, and the door opened. Only it wasn't Dr. Rook, but an alpha female who entered, with dark hair cropped short and a cold expression.

"It's time for your tests," she said.

I recoiled at the mention of *tests*, and her smirk indicated a cruel streak. The word choice had been intended to stir the very reaction I gave.

I wanted nothing to do with her tests, real or imaginary, but I also needed to learn about my new situation. Where was I? How far from the prestigious Varro & Bright offices were we? Was this even Chimera still?

I rose to my feet, doing my best to mask the stiffness and pain from the fall. Instinct told me showing weakness would not serve me well.

I tried to gauge the amount of time that had passed since I walked into the office. Even though I'd been unconscious for a while, I thought it was measured in hours rather than days.

Learning all I could and hoping for the best were both essential, and I would cling to both for as long as possible. Maybe the government was watching this place. Perhaps at any moment, soldiers would storm in and save me from this terrible fate.

"You don't look like him," she said as I drew level.

I stilled. "Who?"

"Gannon."

Was this part of the test? Was I supposed to know this Gannon? "I'm sorry, I don't know that person."

She smirked. "I forgot. He thinks he's so clever. Thetas—victims of their own superiority complex."

I shook my head slowly, eyes shifting toward the corridor beyond the open door where we remained at an impasse.

"Damien Winters," she said, and I felt the blood drain from my face. "Your brother, and master manipulator. We have worked with him for quite a while." She smiled, one that didn't reach her eyes. "Oh, he doesn't know that we know his real name. They use software to change their faces and tone of voice, but we've found ways of unscrambling it. The thetas are willing to do anything to bring the alphas down and claim their moment of power. We help each other, but the cause is too important for chances. We needed leverage, and here you are, falling so perfectly into our laps." Her ice-cold fingertips trailed down my cheek before grasping my chin cruelly. "A pretty little gamma who likes to suck delta cock. We've had our eyes on your men for a while. Such perfect opportunities are rare and must be capitalized upon."

Bile rose in my throat, and I swallowed to force it back down.

"I don't believe that," I said.

"Which part? Your brother? The deltas? It doesn't matter what you think, not at all. In fact, nothing you say or do matters beside your usefulness to the cause. You will behave, or we will find ways to make you. We have a range of inventive ways discovered through our extensive experimental programs. We're not constrained by rules like the Empire, which give us a certain freedom. You can learn a lot that way."

I thought this little talk served no purpose besides terrifying me and setting the expectations of my life swiftly and comprehensively, better propelling me into an obedient worker for the cause.

My throat still turned to dust, and my eyes stung with tears I refused to allow to fall.

She wasn't lying about any of this.

She hated me, hated the Empire, and wanted to control my brother and mates.

My foolish, foolish brother.

I remembered that strange conversation with him, where he'd warned me about taking off world work. What he hadn't done was warn me about speaking to recruiting companies of any kind.

Damien, what have you done to us?

Chapter Twenty-Two

Jordan

It had been a year since we'd met Governor Brach in person. It didn't do to have a couple of criminal enforcers hanging out with the ruling elite. The message was cryptic but gave enough away that we knew it was connected to Abby's disappearance.

We needed answers, but Lucian had nothing to give us. Short of combing the streets or breaking into the Varro & Bright offices, which was still on the table, Victor Brach might just have something.

He did—Abby's older brother in a secure, top-secret underground prison.

I wanted to beat the prick unconscious. I wanted to work through every interrogation technique I knew, call up Ryker, who I was sure had a few more, and then work through them as well.

Except I could do none of them because I wasn't running

this show, and if we wanted Abby back, we needed to play the long game.

At my side, Kade seethed with the same rage. We were connected since mating Abby. What he felt, I felt. What I experienced, so did he.

"You will work for us," Victor Brach said to the pitiful theta slumped against the cold metal walls.

"As a double agent?" Damian Winters asked. He had a slim build and dark hair like Abby, but different eyes. I could see some family resemblance, but not a lot. Then there was something deeper, under the surface, that separated them like mile-wide gulf.

"Yes, exactly that," Brach said. His daughter had been abducted twice. It was fair to say the man wasn't feeling patient with the thetas and their plans to claim control over the empire and displace the alphas. There was a reason the alphas were on top. They were intelligent and physically superior to every other dynamic, save deltas and zetas, but to be fair, zetas were just plain freaks.

"What makes you think you can trust me?" Damien asked. The man was out of options. It was a case of toeing the line with Brach or facing a swift death, probably a fake suicide, and his connections with the Uncorrupted tossed into the mix.

"I don't," Brach said. A big imposing alpha, he dominated the room. He'd been in the military briefly, but he was always heavier on the intelligence than the brawn. "Which is why ninety percent of your considerable assets will become the property of the government indefinitely. We always appreciate private sector investment."

"You can't do that!" Damien objected. I'd seen men with their spirits broken, and he had every tell. Abby was missing. He understood her connection to him was part of her being targeted.

"You plotted to overthrow us." Brach punctuated each word, voice rising. "You played a part in my daughter's abduction!" He paused, heaving a breath, getting his fury under control. "You could always flee and join the Uncorrupted. That option is available to you."

"You'll let me go?"

Brach shrugged. "You're a danger to us here, one we're prepared to manage for intelligence. There will be conditions, but I don't believe you wish to join them. That's not your aim in all this, is it?"

Damien's sneer held a little spirit, but the wariness returned as his eyes shifted to me.

"You're a dangerous man, Damien. Not just for alphas, but for all dynamics, even thetas. You thought you could control the Uncorrupted, that they would offer you the Empire when we were gone." He huffed out a breath. "They won't. You put your own sister, your family, and the lives of billions upon billions of people at risk for a power play. I ought to let the deltas at you, but they have more important things to take care of."

Damien's lips trembled, just enough to stop me from stalking over there, ignoring Brach's plans to use him as a spy, and beating the shit out of him.

Abby wouldn't want me to, which was the only thing staying my hand.

At least the Abby I knew wouldn't.

She'll still be our Abby, Kade said, and his support wrapped around me, anchoring me when the potent emotions, the fear, threatened to spill out. *Keep that on tap, buddy. Got to get our girl out.*

"Chopper is incoming," Brach said, turning to us. "Do what you've got to do. You have our full support."

I nodded.

Kade nodded.

We were up.

Chapter Twenty-Three

Jordan

We'd worked for the government for years and never once called in a favor or asked them for anything. We hadn't had to ask Brach this time, either. No, he'd understood and had volunteered all we needed.

The Uncorrupted wanted us as well as Abby. It was in the government's interest to aid us, even knowing the risks, because if they didn't, we'd have gone anyway and damned with the consequence. No one messed with an alpha and his mate, and the same rules applied to deltas.

We would do everything we could to mitigate risks, but the Uncorrupted bastards weren't getting Abby. Whatever it took, whatever the fuck was necessary to get our girl out, we were going to do.

They assigned us a crack team of top soldiers from the pool circulating on Chimera. I'd met Dano a few years back, a big, dark alpha with bright eyes who was known for his dry humor and a broad grin every bit as big as his personality. There was no humor on his face today. Emotions were locked down for the mission ahead.

"The team are loaded and ready," he said, taking my arm in a clasp before slapping his hand against Kade's shoulder as we loaded up into the sleek shuttle courtesy of the government.

"I'm just glad she's still on the planet," I said, taking in the team assembled inside. With a drone, the doors closed, and we lifted toward the sky.

"We'll get her out," Dano said. "No chance this ends any other way."

Dano had been a 2IC last time I met him, reporting to James Hudson. Now he was a team leader with four alphas, two betas, and a young male healer omega reporting to him.

Each of them was decked out in the formfitting black battle gear, helmets tucked under arms, and an impressive arsenal of weapons. Well, except for the healer. Omegas never carried weapons. We'd stripped out of our civilian clothes back at the base and were similarly attired. It felt strange to wear military clothes when we were never officially part of the military and had never been in a war situation. The armor fitted perfectly, both flexible and tough. It felt right and solidified my purpose, as did the weapons we had slipped into the various specifically designed slots. It gave me a sense of the gravity of what would soon go down.

Whatever it takes.

We'd worked with many different people and teams over the years. For Lucien, we'd done a few ops on and off planet where necessary, but we often worked on our own. Today, I appreciated having a team of battle hardened soldiers and an experienced healer around us. Brach had told us that the healer specialized in physical and mind healing.

I hoped to hell we wouldn't need his skills for either reason.

Abby had been in their hands for close to twenty-four hours —a long fucking time. Five seconds was too long as far as I was concerned.

"Hey, buddy, you doing okay?" Kade asked, putting a hand on my shoulder. There was a softness to his tone, an intimacy in how the words were spoken only for me. For so long, it had been Kade and me. We'd never needed anyone else. When I met his gaze, I saw my own emotions reflected back. We weren't a couple anymore. We had a mate, one we couldn't live without. "We're gonna get her out."

I nodded. We were coming into land. The blood was pumping through my veins as the adrenaline flooded my system. Helmets were slipped on, weapons checked, and the team lined up, ready to unload.

"All communications are down," Dano said. The shuttle rocked slightly as we touched the landing pad. Like all of us, he would have data and combat visuals on his visor. "Building power will be cut in...three, two, one."

You could almost feel the electricity fail, a strange, dull emptiness in the atmosphere.

The shuttle doors slammed open, and we jumped down, jogging straight for the building entrance, where the security doors, normally closed, lay wide open.

As soon as the power went out, emergency protocols came into play, and every door in the building would automatically unlock. It was possible the floors where the Uncorrupted minions where holding prisoners had their own power source and overrides, but we had a gecko loving friend with impressive skills.

"Location?" I said into the comms, my personal one that I could switch to.

"Yep," the Gecko said, all business. *"Popping up on your interfaces now."*

There she was, a little bouncing greet dot. It hit me hard seeing her like that—close, and yet nothing more than a target on the screen.

"Let's go," Kade said.

Two security guards were waiting at the open door, but we were all issued with state-of-the-art, high-powered immobilizers guns. One blast was all it took, and the threats were out cold on the ground.

We met two more security guards inside before we hit the stairwell, taking four flights down.

The fire door was closed but unlocked. Here, we held, waiting for confirmation.

"We are green," Dano said, voice coming through the helmet comms.

We busted through the door and into a white corridor, following the bouncing dot, courtesy of the Gecko. Rhett had supplied us with tiny pieces of cybernetic equipment to use on Sanders and his buddies, tracking devices that could integrate with fabric...or skin. Some might call it deceptive to use one on Abby. Others might say it was bold, especially given she wasn't even our mate at the time. Still, we were deltas, and methods underhand, above board, and everything in between were on the table when staking a claim. Thank fuck we had. Otherwise, we'd have nothing to show she was still in the building, no reason to justify a raid.

That was so long as the Uncorrupted hadn't found the tracker, which the Gecko had assured me they wouldn't, that it was undetectable unless you knew what to look for.

We progressed down the corridor, disabling anyone who stood in our way, slowly closing in on Abby.

Kade

I was shaking right up until the shuttle door opened, and then my hands were deadly calm. The adrenaline kept me laser focused on what needed to be done. My world had narrowed to a single objective, a single woman.

Abby didn't deserve what had happened. She was too fucking trusting, and how could I blame her for that?

I knew what Jordan was feeling. The rage he'd first experienced when we thought she'd been planning to leave us was merely a mask over a deeper pain that we might have driven her to do it.

Only we hadn't.

She'd gone to see Varro & Bright for a knowledge sharing interview—it was all there in her calendar. The Uncorrupted had hacked her account and tried to remove all traces of it, but Rhett had reversed everything they'd done.

I think I might even come to like that gecko loving fucker.

There would be some changes once we got her out, but that was for later, when this was over. Right now, I just wanted to feel her in my arms, safe and untouched.

The corridor degenerated into chaos around us as we moved fast, taking out any opposition. Abby wasn't the only dynamic to be held here. Dano was here to help us lead the op, but another two teams followed directly behind. In short, all the dynamics that had been captured, brought into the offices under one scheme or another, would be liberated from the Uncorrupted's filthy hands.

Uncorrupted personnel were incapacitated using the immobilizers, with no lasting damage except for how they fell, but it was a hell of a lot safer than letting an Uncorrupted minion out. There was too much risk, not just to our safety but to the safety of the other prisoners here.

Coms were down, but they could be brought back up, and fast was the aim. We had targeted the building through necessity, but the Uncorrupted's local operation only occupied two floors. Ground teams would have surrounded the building, and more teams would be deployed to process prisoners and care for civilians.

Jordan and I had one mission, and that was Abby.

It felt like the corridor went on forever. Screaming people, both friendly and foe, threw themselves at us. The occasional pocket of security presented a challenge, but we pushed through, the operational comms and data via the visor keeping us on target.

"Next right," Jordan said.

The door was open, and there she was, wrestling with some alpha bitch, who had her fingers around her throat.

"Back up!" the alpha snarled at us.

Within a split second, I'd taken everything in—the scratches on the alpha's wrists and the blood under Abby's nose.

That alpha bitch was going down.

There was no hesitation as Jordan and I pulled our triggers as one and made two perfect shots—one slamming into the alpha's shoulder, the other dead center of her head.

She dropped, taking Abby with her.

Abby screamed, trying to ward us off. Her glasses were long gone, not that it would help. We were in black, formfitting battle wear, with blacked out helmets and weapons. My baby was terrified.

We holstered our immobilizers.

"We got you covered," Dano said. "Healer is incoming."

Beyond the doorway, the screams were tapering off, just as the passage of troops and healers liberated the prisoners.

I whipped off my helmet, hands out. "It's us, Abby. You're safe, baby."

"No!" she wailed. "You can't be here. You have to leave."

"Fuck! Abby, it's us," Jordan said. I could feel his tension through the bond as we tried to gather her up, get her the fuck away from the alpha bitch as another soldier waded in to put her in cuffs.

Had the bastards broken Abby's mind? Were we too fucking late?

"They are going to capture you too!" She beat at us with her small fists, and we tried to stop her, trying to calm her down. "I love you," she sobbed. "You can't let them get you. You have to leave. Please just go! It's a trap."

She loved us?

She fucking loves us!

"The hell we're going anywhere," Jordan rumbled, ever the surly bastard, despite the raw emotions I sensed ripping through him at her declaration. "We've got ground and air support. No way are we springing this fucking trap."

I pressed in on one side, and Jordan took the other, squishing her between us, where she needed to be to feel safe. "In case you're confused, Abby," I said, trying to keep my fucking head when an avalanche of emotions was bombarding me. "We came here with a full military operation. I just got confirmation through our comms that they have subdued all the enemy. We're going to take you home."

Chapter Twenty-Four

Jordan

I had slept. Couldn't remember the last time I'd slept so well. Maybe never.

I breathed, and the scent of my shower gel filled my nose along with a lighter fragrance that was all woman.

Kade's heavy arm wasn't flung across my waist. Instead, a head covered in messy auburn waves rested against there, with a small hand curled beneath it.

Kade was still here, but there was a woman between us. Our woman.

Our mate.

I breathed deeper. Letting the moment wash over us.

All of us.

Content.

There was no racing in my mind.

No franticness.

The noise would return soon enough. I wasn't deluded that one little gamma could tame the beast inside me in an instant.

But she felt like home.

Like the missing piece.

Like she was always part of us, but we just hadn't found her yet.

Kade shifted, and his arm came around her to settle against me.

I liked that. The weight of them, knowing Abby was thoroughly trapped and safe between us.

Her small hand searched and found Kade's, and their fingers tangled where they rested against me.

When we arrived at our apartment last night, Kade had taken her to the shower to clean the corruption of that place off her. Afterward, she'd refused food and insisted she just wanted to be held. So we held her, all three of us made restless by the magnitude of what had almost come to pass until sleep took us under.

There had been no thoughts toward fucking, but now, as her hand, definitely hers, pushed his downward, my heart rate jacked up, and blood surged into my dick as I realized where those hands were going.

"Hold him for me," she whispered, voice a little sleep slurred.

She rolled onto her knees, pushing the covers aside, and positioned herself between my spread thighs. Kade, only too happy to oblige, scooted down next to her and gave my dick a lazy pump before directing it toward her mouth. Eyes meeting mine, she closed her lips around me, and the head of my cock disappeared into her hot, wet mouth.

Fuck, wasn't I the luckiest bastard in the universe.

Her lips popped off, and she shared a sweet, lusty kiss with Kade before he took a turn sucking the head of my cock.

I nearly blew my fucking load, could barely hold it as they shared a kiss before she sucked me again.

Kisses, sucks, and kisses again. Hands wrapped around my shaft and another set gently rolling my balls.

"I fucking love you two," I said as fierce and all-consuming emotions rose within me. "Fucking love you."

"We both love you," Kade said before taking her lips in a fierce kiss that held so much more than mere words.

We'd nearly lost her.

Now I needed this, needed to remember that we were still here, still free.

"Eat her out while she's sucking me off," I said, voice gruff with the strain. "I want to watch her pretty face while she gets off with her lips wrapped around my cock."

They broke the kiss, breathing in each other's breath before he redirected her to my cock and slid off the bed.

She hummed around me, sucked me deep, and then emitted a long filthy moan. I couldn't see what he was doing, but Kade was a giver and always made it good.

"That feel good, baby?"

She nodded, never taking her lips off me, bobbing her head up and down and swirling her tongue around in a way that had me seeing stars.

I hoped he got her off fast because I wasn't going to last.

"I'm going to come," I gritted out just as she went wild, sucking me deep. Her garbled groans as she got off, hands working my shaft and tongue performing magic, sent me straight after her. My balls tightened, and my mind blanked out to everything but the heady rush of shooting load after load of cum down her willing throat.

Sanity was slow to return. My fingers closed over her hair, drawing her off because she was intent on sucking every drop of cum and then some, and after that blinding climax, I was too sensitive.

She growled at me like an angry kitten.

Chuckling, Kade picked her up and dropped her on her back beside me.

I rolled to face her, cupping her cheek and kissing her, tasting myself on her as Kade crawled over her.

"Was that nice, baby?"

"Yes," she breathed.

"You want Kade inside you now?"

"Yes, god, please."

Kade lined up, and we both watched as his beautiful, fat dick sank slowly in, filling her, stretching her, opening her all up.

The way her neck arched and her face contorted with pleasure lit an echo inside me. The bond, the connection between us, shared emotions and pleasure in equal parts. What they felt, I felt too.

Kade kissed her and then turned to kiss me, then all three of us were breathing heavily, sharing kisses, tangling tongues as he began to thrust, slow and easy inside her.

Abby

I was in heaven. Didn't know a delta could do sweet, but oh, how I needed it, the connection, the sense of us as a three. I'd come too close to losing them, losing everything.

"I love you," I said, kissing Jordan and then Kade. Rich, complex emotions welled up as I accepted what they had recognized from the start.

That they were my soul mates.

That we were one.

That, time and circumstance permitting, I could put my

hands on them as they could put theirs on me, like this, every damn day.

My pleasure rose toward inevitability, despite my desire to stave it off because this was perfect too.

The light slap at the end of each thrust, the tingling deep inside told me Kade was close to hooking me, and an avalanche of pleasure was about to sweep me away.

And then it did, and I was writhing, my moans swallowed by hungry kisses. Pleasure pulsed, deep and endless.

"That's my good girl, Jordan said, lips beside my ear. "You come so sweetly, Abby. Do you know how lucky I feel to have you both in my life? I feel like a fucking king."

His voice broke a little.

This savage male had a softer side, one I thought might take a lifetime to fully reveal.

And Kade, so unique, so giving, so open with his affection and love, and who took pleasure in pleasing us.

They were my wonders.

Kade rolled onto his side, the movement tugging on the hook in the most intensely pleasurable way. Drawing my thigh over his, he opened me up. I nipped at his chest as Jordan slid close behind me and wrapped his arm around Kade, squishing me between them.

I sighed as the slight movements tugged on the hook and sent little sparks through me.

"I'm so glad deltas don't take no for an answer," I said.

Kade chuckled. "'Damn straight we don't take any of your bullshit restraining orders." Cupping my ass, he rocked a little, prolonging the sweet sensations and making me gasp.

"Is that still valid?" Jordan asked Kade.

"Nah, got the Gecko to sort it out."

"So you're friends with the Gecko now?" I said, only half listening to the conversation and quietly basking on my high.

"Friends is a strong word," Jordan said. "I can speak to him without wanting to wrap my fingers around his throat."

"That's real progress," Kade agreed.

"My savage mates." I smiled as I pressed a hand to each of their cheeks. "I love you exactly how you are. Hooks, demons, and all. I should be encouraging you to seek therapy, but please, don't ever change."

Chapter Twenty-Five

Kade

A week later, life was finally returning to something close to normal. Well, as normal as it was going to get, given our line of work and being newly mated to a sweet gamma.

Abby had gone to work today, saying she needed to get back to her clients. I could read between the lines, seeing the tension on her pretty face as much as I could feel through the bond. Still, I understood that her work was important to her and would help her heal after her ordeal to find her purpose again.

Then there was Lucian bemoaning how shit needed our unique skills, but Lucian would have to wait because our other boss had called us first.

Certain parts about Abby's capture and rescue had been playing on my mind. I'd spoken to Jordan about them, and he'd agreed.

We needed some answers.

"You knew what she was going into." Jordan leveled his

accusation on Brach the moment the door closed on the governor's fancy office, a stately room with equally impressive views.

"Not exactly," Brach replied. "We'd had our suspicions but had never followed anyone closely enough to verify."

"You fucking knew," Jordan repeated.

"Is your mate safe?" Brach asked coolly. "Did we get her out? Are twenty-three other dynamics, formerly due to be shipped off planet, also now safe and reunited with their families?"

My hands shook. It wasn't exactly an admission of guilt, nor a denial, just a justification.

Brach was a slippery bastard. The alpha was intelligent, but no one rose to the lofty ranks of the ruling council without being exceptional, even among alphas. I wanted to hate him for putting Abby at risk, which I now believed he had, but as he pointed out, we'd also saved twenty-three dynamics, and it was hard to hold on to anger when all of them were safe.

"We're quitting," Jordan said.

My head swung his way. We hadn't discussed *this*.

Brach huffed out a breath. "You don't get to quit. Nobody quits."

"I'm fucking quitting," Jordan said.

He always spoke for us, even if the asshole should have fucking warned me.

Trust me.

Yeah, right. I was still going to kick his ass in the next training session.

"How about we negotiate," Brach said easily. "Take a vacation."

"There will be no fucking negotiations," Jordan said, eyes doing that twitching thing.

"A little time for you to cool off," Brach continued. "Time

to see that while my approach isn't always virtuous, sometimes it's necessary."

"Not with our mate, it's not."

"If we had known what was happening at Varro & Bright, we'd have gone in already. We didn't. You can make of that what you will."

"Letting Abby go in confirmed it," I pressed.

Brach inclined his head. "It did. Why don't you ask Abby what we should have done?"

"That's not a fair question," I said, feeling sick to my gut, because I knew Abby would have done it.

"The ruling council may be alphas, but that doesn't mean we're the only voices heard. Our advisors are many and from all dynamic castes. Ask an omega what they would have done in such circumstances. Ask a gamma, it's exactly the same. Every one of them would have put their life on the line in the same situation, especially to save others. It goes against everything alpha, every protective instinct we have, and deltas are no different, save for some anatomy. They have the same tempered aggression, the same dominance, and the same all-consuming protective instincts. So these are hard decisions, and for me especially, because I'm an alpha, but I'm on the ruling council for a reason. I run operations like this because they get results. I employ the best and most skilled people for the same reasons. My operations lead to the greater good."

"And what about the risks?" Jordan asked.

"There are always risks," Brach replied. "Every day of our lives, we are at war. In case it has escaped your notice, we've been losing for a very long time, but recently, the tide has started to turn, the scales tipping in our favor. Don't get me wrong—we've a long way to go. If you want to keep your mate safe, your future children safe, don't turn your back on your duty or purpose. I'll give you some time. If you want to resign afterward, I'll even accept it."

Jordan's growl was low but quickly tapered off.

I already knew what our answer would be. I felt it, the acceptance from Jordan, but also from me. We couldn't turn away from this. Brach was right—we needed to make the world safe, not just our world, but all the worlds within the Empire.

Fuck knew how many operations like this Brach was aware of or managing, but it struck me then that there must be very many, that Jordan and I were small but useful cogs that, together with all those other cogs, we could make a difference, could turn the tide, as Brach had said.

We had a purpose and would play our part for Abby, our children, and the thousands of other dynamics who lived under threat.

"I'll take the fucking vacation," Jordan said. "A long one."

Brach's lips tugged up. "A long one," he agreed. "And then I'll expect you to sign in."

We going to trust this asshole? Jordan asked me.

No, but we are going to accept.

"Yes, sir," we both said.

"Excellent," Brach said, smiling like he'd already fucking known. "Dismissed."

In the reception area, his beta personal assistant slid a small communication earbud across the desk toward us.

Jordan picked it up with a huff and slipped it into his pocket

Brach would call us, vacation or not, when he needed us again.

"Come on," Jordan said. "Let's get the fuck out here. I think it's time to show off our mate."

Chapter Twenty-Six

Abby

"I'm not sure about this," I said, smoothing my hands down my pretty black cocktail dress that hugged my curves. Seeing myself without glasses for the first time in my life was also strange. I'd always thought my parents had connections, but Lucian Banner had more. After a safe but incredibly expensive procedure still not available outside the military, my glasses were a thing of the past. The best part? Seeing my lovers up close when we were getting hot and dirty, because glasses and enthusiastic sex really didn't go so well together. "I feel like I'm naked."

Kade's eyes turned to half-mast as he adjusted the cuff on his tailored dark suit before stalking over to me. Slipping an arm around my waist, he lowered his eyes to my cleavage. "Sweetheart, we can stay at home if you like, but this pretty dress may not be fit to wear after, because I'm going to tear it off, bend you over that handy couch that is the perfect height for fucking, and fill you all up."

My heart thumped about in my chest, and my stomach took that slow tumble as arousal pooled deep inside me.

"I, ah..." Where had we been going? My mind had turned alarmingly blank to everything but the image Kade had painted with a few erotic words.

"She looks hot as fuck, and you're not ripping anything from her until I've had a chance to show her off," Jordan said, joining us in the dressing room of their apartment, high above Peppermint Moon. With dark blond hair that fell to his shoulders, a little stubble along his jaw, and eyes the color of liquid mercury, Jordan cut an imposing figure of masculinity in his matching black suit.

Kade brushed his lips against my temple before skimming his knuckles down my throat and across my collarbone, making my breath catch as I willed him to put them somewhere more intimate.

He didn't, and his smirk said he knew what I wanted.

"Fine," Kade agreed. "She doesn't get any dick."

"What! Why?" I exclaimed, turning from Kade to Jordan.

Jordan chuckled. "I swear she craves my cum as much as you do. Neither of you are getting any unless she puts this collar on and does at least one lap of the club."

"The fuck?" Kade muttered. "What did I do?"

"Threatening to bend her over, asshole. You know she'll never leave if you throw offers like that around. Besides, Lucian doesn't give us a night off very often. I'll make it good for both of you later—when I'm ready, and not before."

Kade and I groaned. Jordan always made it good, and the thought of pleasing him got both of us hot.

"Please put it on," I said. I wanted to go. I'd been the one to suggest it after Jordan bought me the dress. I'd never owned anything so beautiful in my life, and the moment I'd slipped it on, I'd felt so good, and I wanted to be brave and be me for once. The real me, the one that felt safe to shine for the first time in my life. I'd even started dressing normally for work, nothing like this, but at least not a smock two sizes too big.

"Hold her hair up," Jordan said, nodding his head at Kade.

That was something else new—hair that skimmed my shoulders. I'd grown it out, I could admit freely, because I liked the feel of their hands pulling it, using it to guide my mouth.

Goodness. "I-I don't think I can wait," I said, a little breathless as the cool strip of black leather was placed around my throat.

"Can't wait for what?" Jordan asked, carefully clipping the collar into place and testing the fit. I'd worn it around the house a few times and loved how it made me feel. This was also my first time wearing it outside.

"You, both of you. Please."

"You want cock, sweetheart?" Kade asked.

"Yes, please. Yes, I want...cock." I said it because they liked me to say it. No mortifying word could be omitted when I made a request, or they pretended not to understand me. Deltas, I'd discovered, were both cruel and wicked.

"Not happening," Jordan said, lips tugging up in a rare smirk, one I'd come to crave as much as his touch. Hand resting on my shoulder, he turned me around. "On your knees, Kade. Our mate needs something to give her a little buzz while we are out and to keep her focused on being a good girl for us."

My heart did that little *ba-dump*.

Kade grinned. "My pleasure." He sank down before me and lifted my dress up.

"Part your pretty thighs for him," Jordan said, voice low and growly beside my ear.

"What are you—Oh," I muttered weakly as Kade pressed his nose to my panties and licked me through the silky material.

"Is she wet?" Jordan asked, big hand enclosing the front of my throat.

"Let's check," Kade said. Hooking a finger in my panties, he drew them aside and used his thumbs to open me up. "Pink, pretty, and very wet. Let me clean you all up, sweetheart, so you're comfortable. Can't have you going out like this."

"Oh god." At the first swipe of his tongue, I was panting.

"Don't get her off," Jordan said.

Kade and I groaned, but he didn't get me off, just teased me until I was desperate, then we went out. I was so damn needy that all I could think about was getting my cookie. Hellbent on stoking my arousal ever higher, they found inventive ways to put their hands on me, tease me, kissing, pinching, and petting. At one point, Jordan stopped to talk to some friends. After introducing me, Kade dragged me to a shadowy corner. Here, he closed his lips over mine for a drugging kiss, lifted my dress, slipped a single finger under the seam of my panties, and then teased me until I was begging. Jordan found us and peeled him off me with a shake of his head.

We enjoyed a drink and a dance. The music thumped, full of bass, and the lights flashed over the dance floors but were subtle everywhere else. The atmosphere pulled me in, while my two men, one or both of them ever at my side, kept reminding me with a look or touch that I was the center of their world.

I loved every moment of being with them, close to them, their eyes holding mine in a way that showed me that the connection thrumming between us was perfect in every way. It was the reason I'd never given up when life had seemed so very dark.

By the time Jordan finally called it time, Kade and I were panting like a couple of teenagers. I'd left marks over his throat and had ranked my fingers through his dark hair so many times, it was sticking up all over the place.

In the elevator, Jordan and Kade kept me sandwiched between them, where I arched and twitched and got frustrated when they wouldn't give me more.

Then we were back at their apartment—a place that had been their home long before I came on the scene—and the tension exploded inside me until I felt like I'd caught on fire.

Jordan shrugged out of his jacket, tossed it over a nearby chair, and sat back on the couch. He gestured toward the couch opposite.

Jacket and shoes off. I want to watch you making out like the world is ending tomorrow.

Kade and I fell on one another with searching hands and lips, all the while knowing Jordan was watching, feeling his arousal through the bond. I found myself straddling Kade's lap, my neckline down with his mouth on my breast, my skirt up, and panties down, stretched wide around my thighs. As his thick fingers toyed with my slippery clit, I was fast approaching the point of no return.

Fuck her, now.

I was blind to the world, to everything but Jordan's commands booming through the bond, making the hairs across the surface of my skin tingle.

The world turned. I was facedown over the couch, cheek pressed into soft leather. Deep, aroused growls and the jangle of a belt were my only warning before a thick cock was pushed against my slippery pussy and thrust inside.

I groaned, already feeling myself fluttering on the brink of bliss, while Kade had one hand squeezing a breast and the other cupping my pussy, fingertips pressing over my clit oh so lightly, holding me everywhere and inside all at once.

Hold it.

I sensed as much as felt Jordan coming down behind Kade, then my pussy clenched wildly as I understood what he was about to do—fill Kade while Kade was filling me.

I *felt* the savage penetration like it was happening to me, making me feel full everywhere—body, heart, and mind.

"This is going to get rough." Jordan grunted. "You with me, little mate? You ready for a good, deep hooking, the kind that has you seeing stars?"

"God, yes please. Don't hold back."

He didn't. Hot flesh stroked me deeply as grunts, growls, and heavy groans filled the air. I gave a sharp cry as they hooked, then felt the pulsing waves of bliss, the hot flood inside, and a tingling pleasure that never let go.

Here, with my savage lovers, I had found my own heaven.

About the Author

Thanks for reading *Savage Control*. Want to read more? Check out the rest of my Controllers series and my other books!
Amazon: https://www.amazon.com/author/lvlane

Where to find me...
Website: https://authorlvlane.com
Blog: https://authorlvlane.wixsite.com/controllers/blog
Facebook: https://www.facebook.com/LVLaneAuthor/
Facebook Page: https://www.facebook.com/LVLaneAuthor/
Facebook reader group: https://www.facebook.com/groups/LVLane/
Twitter: https://twitter.com/AuthorLVLane
Goodreads: https://www.goodreads.com/LVLane

Also by L.V. Lane

Prey

I am prey.

This is not pity talking, this is an acknowledgment of a fact.

I am small and weak; I am an omega. I am a prize that men war over.

For a year I have hidden in the distant corner of the Empire.

But I am running out of food, and I am running out of options.

That I must leave soon is not a decision for today, though, but a decision for tomorrow.

Only tomorrow's choices never come.

For tonight brings strangers who remind me that I am prey.

Prey is a fantasy reverse harem Omegaverse with three stern alphas, an alpha wolf-shifter, and a stubborn omega prey.

Printed in Great Britain
by Amazon

19468002R00135